ଔ

HUMAN PERSONALITY IS LIKE RELIGION. It can be a source of great wisdom and solace, but it also creates divisions, conflicts, and sometimes even wars. Personalities, like religions, had often done more harm than good, and now that more than sex was involved, now that our personalities had entered into the relationship, we were already experiencing conflict. IT WAS OH SO MUCH EASIER WHEN FEW WORDS WERE EXCHANGED AND ALL WE DID WAS FUCK.

EROTOMANIA

∝ A ROMANCE ∞

A NOVEL BY
FRANCIS LEVY

TWO DOLLAR RADIO
Since*2005

Visit **www.ErotomaniaRomance.blogspot.com**

Cover photograph by Frans de Waal.
Cover design by Two Dollar Radio.

Published by the Two Dollar Radio Movement, 2008.
Copyright 2007 by Francis Levy.

ISBN: 978-0-9763895-7-6
LCCN: 2008900721
All rights reserved.
First Printing.

ᏸ

Distributed to the trade by Consortium Book Sales & Distribution, Inc.
The Keg House
34 Thirteenth Avenue NE, Suite 101
Minneapolis, Minnesota 55413-1007
www.cbsd.com phone | 612.746.2600 | fax 612.746.2606
orders 800.283.3572

Two Dollar Radio
Book publishers since 2005.
"Because we make more noise than a $2 radio."
www.TwoDollarRadio.com
twodollar@TwoDollarRadio.com

NOTE ON THE COVER PHOTOGRAPH. This photograph of two copulating bonobos was taken by Frans de Waal. Bonobos and chimpanzees, which are related to each other, are our closest primate relatives. Bonobos are also known as the "make love, not war" primates, as they show very little violence and have lots of sex. It used to be thought that face-to-face sex was uniquely human.

—Photograph by **Frans de Waal,**
author of *Our Inner Ape*

૦ૐ

AUTHOR'S ACKNOWLEDGEMENT. I want to thank Maggie Paley for her insight, humor, and constant patience in helping me to edit the manuscript. I would also like to thank Eliza and Eric Obenauf for their their neverending fund of energy, creativity, and resourcefulness as editors and publishers. Thanks also to Adam Ludwig for his editorial suggestions, Patricia McCormick for being an inspired advocate, and to my wife Hallie Cohen for her loving and unforgiving critical eye.

ଔ

For Hallie, Zeno, and Titus

EROTOMANIA

❧ A ROMANCE ☙

༼ష

I GAVE HER A GOOD FUCK, WALKED OUT, AND HAD A FEW BEERS at the corner bar. It wasn't one of my hangouts; I didn't know anybody, but I didn't care. I still smelled of her pussy, I felt I owned the place. She had a boyfriend who came home from work at ten, but I would have left anyway. I didn't like talking to her, but I loved the way she fucked. She fucked as the Anna Magnani figure in Rossellini's *Open City* (1945) would have fucked—devouring her partner like a child stealing sweets. Neither of us bothered with the niceties. I'd pull her blouse over her head. She'd unzip my fly and go down on me. It was after we were through that the trouble began. I always found myself wandering in the street, not remembering her face or how it had started. We'd stopped fucking at 9:01. I noticed it on her digital clock. By 9:04 I was already putting my socks on. I always put my socks on before putting on my underwear and jeans since her floors were so cold. They were made of marble. The bedroom was in what had once been the bathroom of an old mansion that was now split up into apartments, but no one had ever dealt with the heating system, which was probably another reason she liked having one more body on top of her during the evening than she would have had, if she'd been faithful to her boyfriend. I was like that extra blanket you keep at the bottom of the bed to make sure you get enough heat.

The little bit of talk she insisted on as I pulled my pants off was a formality, and I hated her for it since she had nothing to say. The forced talking was where the prostitution came in. A person has to pay for his pleasures; it's the Protestant Ethic. I don't see why people just can't accept the fact that they're going to fuck, that there is no rhyme or reason for the fucking, that it doesn't need to be lily-coated or explained away with good intentions. You don't insist on the niceties when you breathe or sit down to take a crap. Okay, fucking involves another person, and there are fucks that can be accompanied by meaningful conversation, but it's not *post hoc, ergo propter hoc.* One doesn't necessarily follow from the other.

I stopped for pizza on the way home. Normally I would have felt sorry for myself eating alone in the pizzeria on Chapel Street a week before Christmas, but I'd been fucked and I knew I didn't want anything more for the moment. It wasn't just that I'd been fucked, it was all the memories of how much she wanted me and how wantonly she pursued her orgasms. She placed her finger against my asshole. It was like putting a key in the ignition. She had control of me, guiding me back and forth over her. She was selfish in the pursuit of pleasure. The extent of her desire made me question the meaning of human love. I remembered a scene of a hyena chasing down a baby kangaroo on "Wild Kingdom." It was feasting on the kangaroo's intestines, its mouth covered with blood, even as the creature's limbs were still moving.

This wanting me—especially since we plainly didn't care about each other's well being in all the usual ways—made me doubt everything. Was the feasting on each other, like animals on the steppe, the true essence of the man/animal? I drink my beer, I eat my pizza, I take my crap, I go to sleep, I get up, go over and fuck her brains out before the boyfriend comes home from work. That would be tomorrow, the next day, and the day after. I wasn't complaining. I didn't want anything else out of life. I had just never experienced human selfishness in such a raw and appealing form.

She wanted me because of the way my dick unselfconsciously rammed both her holes, and I liked how she thrust her tongue in my mouth as she drove her nails into my back. As I impaled her, she thrashed about just like that kangaroo. What were all these other relationships with their medical policies, their certificates, their insurance, their pre- and postnuptial agreements, their fights, their consultations, their counseling sessions, their birthdays, their anniversaries and burials, their picture albums, pendants? Candlelight talks at restaurants whose architecture created the appropriate mood to induce fornication lacked the bare-bones truthfulness of our fucking, which in this last incarnation even included some hair pulling. She placed my hand on the hair at the back of her head as I fucked her in the ass. Having been given the reins, I was yanking on her mane. She screamed. I couldn't tell if it was out of pleasure or pain. She was now a galloping horse. I was pulling on the bit. What was I learning?

I couldn't get the taste of her out of my mouth despite the fact that I'd ordered my pizza with pepperoni and pepper. I'm a tolerant man, I'll put up with anything but the pretension to romantic love. It's almost as bad as the self-congratulatory pretension to culture that you see amongst opera-goers. If she'd only shut her mouth when I was getting dressed, I could take the mildewed taste of her pussy in my mouth forever.

Our encounters weren't all nonverbal communications or perfunctory chatter. There were a few great recitatives before we got carried away on her lubricity and my hardness. For instance, soon after I walked in I said *you look like you really want to get fucked today*, which was matched by her *yeah my cunt is really hot and empty. I want you to shoot over my face, all over my lips and nose and cheeks, I want it dripping from my eyelids then fuck me hard in the ass.* The only fight we ever had was when I took the talking too far. I said *imagine me taking a hot piss between your tits.* We were actually already fucking when I said that because sometimes we talked dirty to each other while we were in the process. She stopped in the middle of everything. *Take that back. I don't like that.* I thought she was going to pull herself out from under me, but a few seconds later she gave me the green light by shoving her finger up my ass again.

Who was she? She was just this girl I met on the street. I didn't pick her up. In essence, it's every man's fantasy: You spot a babe, she asks if you want to come up to her place. I had my tongue in her mouth and my finger in her hole within three or four minutes of appraising the premises. There were no lines, no enchantment, no seduction. There was no dialogue. I didn't make any comments about the architecture of her apartment or the provenance of any of its furnishings. I displayed a distinct unknowledgeability. For someone who was so desired, I was immediately impressed by how unimportant I appeared to be. I'm not the kind of charismatic character women flock to. Yet she wanted me without my saying anything pithy, romantic, insightful, or empathetic. She definitely was not after me because I possessed insight about her which others lacked. I knew nothing. Emotion is supposed to lead to sex. In our case the sex preceded emotion. I could have been watching a porn flick. Instead I was living it and watching it at the same time. Why try for more when everything was so perfect? If I got to know her history, her problems, defeats, joys, infatuations, it could be a disaster for our lovemaking.

Sitting in the pizza place with a shit-eating grin on my face, I smelt the legacy of our fuck, but I didn't miss *her* when I wasn't with her. I missed having that experience in my life for the hours between our meetings, but I felt no need to communicate with her. Therein lay one of the true mysteries of our relationship. Since I didn't participate in the usual idealization, since I had no feeling of being incomplete without her, there was no drive to be with her. I didn't look for her on the street, I didn't hope to run into her, neither did I imagine myself turning away so as not to greet her at a particular moment because I would at that moment fall short of the ideal image she had of me.

What brought us back to each other? Animal memory is based on presence. A dog will run to his master, but from the neurological point of view he doesn't have the ability to retain the image of his master when the master is not proximate. This is supposedly what separates man from beast, the process of subjectivization by which image is turned into memory (the price for this ability is that man is deprived of a certain truth since these retained memories are all filtered through the distorting lens of consciousness). The infant's ability to retain the image of the mother is one of the things that allows for separation. I'm human. Naturally, I was fully capable of imagining her, but I didn't. The electricity generated between us occurred only when we were in each other's presence, but—and this is the key—it was far greater than any romantic passion created by thought. I became an animal in a man's body, a centaur, a creature out of mythology who was like a man in his capacity for retrospection and an animal in his acts. But still, under the circumstances, what brought us together?

From the day I found myself lying on her bed with what would become the ritual of her nails in my back followed by the gentle prodding of my anus, I have been filled with the same sense of wonder. How did I get here? Was our fucking the product of some healing force of nature existing multi-dimensionally and at the same time surreptitiously—a hidden vein in the universe that the right collocation of moon, suns, stars, of micro or macro particles of multi- and mini-verses had suddenly unleashed in us? Would it end just as it had started, without drama, forethought, or explanation? Would the magnetic pull one day cease to exist to such an extent that I might find myself in her presence wondering how I could ever have fucked her, wondering how I could have licked and touched, literally wined and dined on such foul-smelling meat? Beyond being the most pleasurable thing in my life, she was nothing to me. If the magic left, we would have no history. There would be nothing to talk about, to reminisce about, no standard of comparison by which I would hold this relationship up to any other, unless I were to read off a succession of sexual events, one remarkably similar to the other—and I wonder about my access to these fragments. Without the reality of the memory of a person, is it still possible to relive a passion? And if not, is it possible I would receive no payback for all my effort, nothing to immortalize the heights to which she and I had ascended?

I had been so hungry that I burned my tongue on the pizza. The cold Corona I drank with it didn't help matters. Sometimes when you try to salve a pain you make it worse. Despite the burn, I was still hungry, but everything in town closes up by eleven except for the pizzerias and the all-night diner. If I'd had a car I would have driven out to Route 1 with its line of KFCs, McDonald's, Wendy's, and Burger Kings, which stay open late into the night. I got voraciously hungry after our fucks. After all, they were a workout, but this time, my hunger notwithstanding, I was also infected with wanderlust. I couldn't bear to return home with some garlic knots from yet another pizzeria or the fries I'd find in the all-night diner, and turn on the television— which was what I'd done with the rest of the evening after our previous encounters. I felt claustrophobic just thinking about it. I couldn't simply plunk myself down on my sofa and stuff my face. The Greyhound Terminal was only ten blocks away and it had dispensers with candy, potato chips, and soda, which would be enough to stave off my appetite until I could decide if I actually wanted to hop on a bus and go somewhere.

It was as if someone were shoving me. I fell forward and before I knew it I was being hit in the head. I took the two figures in, but I was too scared to look at their faces. Curiously, I remarked to myself how well they plied their craft. There was a crunching sound that I later realized was my elbow hitting the ground—after a left hook found the side of my head. They started kicking me and calling me a "geek." I said, "I didn't do anything. I'm not who you think I am," before I lost consciousness. I don't know how long I was out. When I awakened, a couple of the methadone addicts who linger in the shadows of Chapel Street were standing over me. I couldn't move my arm and I was sure they were going to rifle through my pants, but they didn't. I recognized the heavyset one with the belly that stuck out over his belt. A lot of the addicts talk loudly as if they've lost the ability to modulate their voices. Of all of them, he was the most notorious.

"You want us to call the cops?"

"A lot of good that will do, but yes." I felt in my pants and pulled out my wallet. The thugs hadn't taken any money. It made no sense. I guess that's why they call it a shit-eating grin. I'd been just a little too happy with myself. Now instead of feeling complacent, relatively carefree, I wanted help. If I'd known her number I might have called, but we'd never exchanged numbers. All we'd done in all our times together was fuck. Besides, her boyfriend was likely to pick up.

A police car rolled to the curb where I was sitting. The two cops inside were slow to get out. The methadone addicts were always getting beaten up, and one of them had been hit by a cab the week before when she nodded out while crossing Chapel. I figured the cops thought I was one of them. My elbow seemed to be hanging out of its socket, but it didn't hurt as long as I supported it with my other arm. I still wanted to board a bus, but I consented to get in the police car to look for the two guys who'd beaten me up. We cruised around the block once and then once again. The cops asked me to describe my assailants, but I was tongue-tied. *They looked like you two guys, big husky white guys of Italian origin. They looked like your relatives.* I didn't say it, and when they'd finished with the obligatory tour, they gave me a card with the precinct's phone number and told me to call if I had anything to add. They left me off at the bus station, where I acquired two bags of Wise potato chips and a Diet Coke. Eating and drinking I found were a problem unless the arm was supported.

I was sitting on a bench, really a series of flimsy red plastic chairs welded together. The bus station was filled with homeless people trying to look purposeful, playacting the part of travelers. These homeless had an almost frenetic air, moving back and forth between the varying gates so that they wouldn't be evicted from the warmth of the station by the ubiquitous security guards, but opposite me sat a desolate character who had given up. He sat perfectly still, staring at his feet. Another group of homeless men had momentarily congregated around a column. The guards were edging them away with their clubs. He would be next. A solitary shopping bag was wedged between his legs. Some of the others were wheeling shopping carts filled to the top with coats, pans, books, and boxes of cereal (many of the homeless inhabiting the station seemed to love Sugar Smacks). At least he didn't have much to carry.

"Pssst… psst." He didn't look up. "Eh, they're gonna nail you. C'mon, don't just sit there like a stooge."

He was totally motionless. It's hard to institutionalize anyone these days with the new laws, but they have a heyday with the catatonic cases. I hoped he had a lot to think about—if that is what goes on when someone is in this kind of state of mind—because with cases like his they lock you up and throw away the key.

I have this thing about confinement. My mother died of Parkinson's disease when I was a freshman in college. The legendary beauty who'd introduced me to the joys of French kissing had become an old crone who spit up over herself like an infant. I didn't think much about the ramifications while she was ebbing away. I'd watch a little television with her in whatever hospital room she was occupying and I was out of there—usually running to hookers or the dilapidated movie theaters where the X-rated films played in those days. I'd literally run from the hospital. It was only after she died that I realized the same thing might happen to me, if I carried the wrong gene. I was a little late, but in my fear I began to empathize with her pain. I saw myself locked up in my own body. Now that's even worse than being locked in a jail cell or a ward. You can't even scratch yourself. You can't move when you need to. It started to come back to me how uncomfortable she was—the stiff necks, the soreness in her buttocks from sitting all day, the stiffness in her side and back. You could barely hear her complaints. She mumbled under her breath; sometimes I pretended I couldn't hear. I'd kill myself if I got it.

I snagged my friend by his collar and literally pulled him up off the bench. One of the guards saw what was going on out of the corner of his eye, but he turned away. They'd jump at any excuse to avoid having to deal with the fighting and the stink since most of these homeless shit and pissed in their pants. No one wants to use a stick on someone who is helpless or insane, though it happens all the time. Once the guards in the bus station started hitting these creatures, they vented their frustration on them and there was blood everywhere. That's why people were staying away from the Greyhound Terminal. It could erupt on a moment's notice.

My friend started to whimper. There'd been a rash of gruesome murders in which homeless men had been suffocated and tortured. He had his wits about him enough to be scared.

"I'm not trying to hurt you. Trust me. I'm just going to take you over to my pad. You can take a shower and eat. You don't have to say anything, though my advice to you is to start spilling it. All you have to do is talk and you stay off the locked ward. Talking's like a passport."

I couldn't move my elbow. But I was able to get Bill back to my apartment, where the three S's—shave, shit, shower—became my primary concern for him, considering my new friend's appearance and smell. I was about to make him a sandwich when he looked in my refrigerator, identified himself as a cook, and offered to fix us a snack. Considering my condition, I was in no position to refuse.

What he set out on the table wasn't a snack, it was a work of art. He told me he'd been the chef on the 125-foot yacht of a retired real estate mogul and he'd been fired for drinking. His wife had already left him, but his last bender, a three-day jaunt that took him from Disney World to Palm Springs, had cost him his girlfriend, his house, and the custody of his only child. He'd wanted to kill himself, but he didn't have the guts. He was waiting for someone to do it for him. I quickly informed Bill I wasn't volunteering for the job, but if he'd like a place to stay, I'd be glad to trade the living room couch for his promise to cook me an occasional meal.

Bill's face lit up. The transformation was miraculous. I could barely recognize him; there was hardly any resemblance to the derelict I'd found in the bus station. He took me to the emergency room and waited four hours with me so a resident could snap what turned out to be a dislocated elbow back into place.

ଔ

Our first formal dinner was vegetarian chili. I had just come back from fucking her and I was starving. Bill's presentation was as beautiful as the food. Little bowls of condiments—Monterey Jack, olives, sour cream, chutney—surrounded the chili. There was a tossed salad and fresh baked corn bread. Her smell was still on me, and the residue of the chili and condiments on my breath left me with the most agreeable case of body odor I'd ever suffered from.

I'd gone momentarily blind during our fucking. I think my brain was hit by an electrical storm. The sensation was so long and intense that I'd fried my synapses. It was like a short circuit. I'd panicked. I'd started to scream.

My father used to tell me you went blind from masturbating, but he didn't tell me a good fuck had an adverse affect on the eyesight. In fact, in the last few weeks since we'd been at it, I'd noticed my nearsightedness had increased.

I was finding myself inside of her, not remembering until after our fucking was over how I'd gotten there. I didn't think of her face. I thought about the inside of her cunt, which was like a person. It pulsed, grabbing my dick and sucking it in. I'd once been to the volcano at the top of the Big Island of Hawaii. There are steam vents, and by the shoreline there are places where you can actually watch the lava streaming into the sea. Lava and steam—that's how I imagined the inside of her cunt. I vaguely recalled the dream of a pert little face with a tiny nose and short cropped dirty blond hair. Was it her?

I never saw her naked. We skipped the burlesque of lovemaking. We were entwined in each other's arms before any exhibitionism could come into play. So I didn't even know what her cunt looked like on the outside. When she was ready to come, she started to buck her hips up into the air; it was effortless, a form of seeking that was its own reward. She wasn't working to get her orgasm as so many women did. It wasn't something she felt she deserved. It wasn't a way of allaying the frustration she would have felt at not being able to come. I was never with her, in fact, when she didn't come many times, screaming, digging her nails into my back and pounding my spine with her fists. It was as if her body knew what it had to do, as if it were programmed for ecstasy. Her fucking was like childbirth.

I felt like one of those mummies in the horror films, who walks out of his casket in the middle of the night in response to a secret word or phrase. In my case I would hear the word "fuck," though as far as I know nobody had said it—the one extrasensory verbal manifestation of the paranormal phenomenon by which we sought each other out. It was as if the pheromones that enabled me to follow her scent also excited the part of the brain that gives language to basic drives. I was a somnambulist, carried through the streets of her neighborhood as if in a dream, with the word echoing in my head.

One night, when her boyfriend was switched to the late shift, I didn't get home until two in the morning. Bill started to heat up the dinner he had cooked—pork loin in barbecue sauce, one of the best things he did. Bill had all the receipts for the meal spread out on the kitchen counter. He'd become my brains, my memory, the face I saw as I sought oblivion in her cunt.

"I've still got some Sky Miles, and I'm thinking of going down to the Keys for a few days," he said.

Immediately I felt a shot of anxiety in my stomach. I wasn't prepared for Bill leaving. I'd come to depend on his meals. We didn't talk much, but I'd gotten used to him being there. It was like having a parent at home when you came in from school. I was already feeling possessive of Bill, but I didn't want to show it. I had to be cool. If I got nervous, he'd start to feel trapped. I'd thought he was happy, grateful, and desperate. I'd overestimated the latter. Here was a guy on desolation row who turned out to have enough credit card points for a lovely vacation.

"Why don't you come? We can stay at the Casa Marina. One of the sous-chefs is my oldest friend. He'll put us up. I may even have enough points to fly us down business class."

But what about her? Her cunt needs to get regularly fucked....

I have to say, I have many faults, but I'm not inconsiderate. I was taking the soft hairy thing between her legs into account. I know what it's like to have an itch. It starts out as physical, but soon turns into a metaphysical longing in which the sufferer never quite feels at home. I started to think about it. Though I still hadn't seen her, I knew her cunt was big and had large labia. I've been with women with oversized clits. Hers, however large and sensitive, was easily buried by her large mass of pubic hair. It's lucky my dick was so hard when we fucked. Half-tumescence would never have penetrated her dense Venus mound. Part of the joy of fucking her was this feeling of conquering uninhabited wilderness. There was the waiting hotness underneath the hairs that lubricated them and my dick. Then one-two-three and I'd made it through, but it was just that feeling of breaking something down that made our fucking so unusually exhilarating. When I think of parting, I imagine sorrow written on a face, but now I saw her big hairy cunt awkwardly desolate, like a precocious child in a boring class—her cunt in the prime of its life, languishing away.

I thought about Bill's offer, weighing it against the relationship. The fact was I had no relationship. I was the victim of a compulsion that I almost wanted to escape. Call it chance, the werewolf phenomenon by which man is turned momentarily into beast; we'd managed to sniff each other out like hounds. The whole thing was a great wet dream which I hadn't yet dealt with as a reality in my life. And with the exception of avoiding the boyfriend (the one area where reason magically came into play), the temporary amnesia that afflicted me before and after each event, making it impossible to remember how I'd come or gone from her bed, only increased the air of unreality. In addition, I wasn't plagued by any work commitments, which is one of the reasons I had the time to indulge my compulsion to be with her in the first place. I'm a set designer for the road productions of Broadway musicals, but my next assignment, *Annie* in Des Moines, was weeks away. I accepted Bill's offer and found myself on a flight to Key West.

Bill warned me that when he and his buddy got going, they could talk about food all night. The chit-chat about fritters, cornmeal, jalapeno pepper stew, and Kentucky boar was a refreshing break from the obsession that had begun to rule my life. The food talk was almost meditative. As the conversations proceeded, my mind was temporarily freed from thoughts of her. Our first night we actually had dinner in the kitchen of the Casa Marina, where Bill's friend, Sam, cooked. We sat on stools by the counter, giggling like a pair of schoolboys. As Sam created dishes, he made hors d'oeuvre-sized samples for us. There was cockle lasagna and steamed calamari jambalaya, smoked prime ribs and lamb innards.

When Sam suggested we hit one of Key West's many strip clubs when he was done with work, I worried about the embarrassing accident that was likely to occur if some beauty sat on my lap. The dancers would reawaken the hyper-sexuality that had been tempered by conversation. Sam's mother was French, and though he'd been raised in Cleveland, he was an avid student of Derrida, Baudrillard, and the French deconstructionists. We'd no sooner entered the dance establishment than the discussion about erotics started. The dancers were all culturally bound representations. Naked breasts and even cunts have absolutely no significance in shamanistic societies. In fact, nudity as a concept only existed in proto-capitalist trade and barter societies, where the taking off of one's clothes was a source of power or humiliation depending on how it was perceived. Sexuality has nothing to do with the body as an image. Biologically, sexual intercourse occurs without any ideation. The sexuality of animals is free from any concepts of masculinity or femininity. The discussion continued as a tall brunette sat on my lap. When I told her I was on a vacation from an intense sexual relationship which had left me in an abnormally stimulated state, she gently lifted herself off me before our relationship got off the ground.

There was a black dancer wearing nothing but thigh-high boots with stiletto heels. She wrapped her arms around a bleached blonde with small breasts and purple pubic hair. They started kissing. The black dancer, who had large pendulous breasts, sat down and lowered her partner into her lap, laying the nipple of her breast on the blonde's mouth. Thereafter followed a scene that reminded me of a Giotto fresco of Jesus in the Virgin Mary's arms. How different this was from the ecstasies of my recent fucking! It had obviously been all choreographed in advance. I'd never realized how much thinking could go into sex. I turned to Sam.

"Sex is actually one of the great intellectual activities, yet everyone mistakenly thinks it's physical. It actually has little to do with instinct. It's all about mind and imagination. And yes, I would agree with you, it's culture bound."

"But the whole Eurocentric critic, the dead white males stuff is passé even with the French," Sam pointed out. He was about to continue when the black girl pulled her head out of the blonde's crotch and leaned backwards, arching her body up in the air and supporting herself by her hands. She was staring at Sam's face. She licked her lips and then flicked her tongue suggestively.

"How much for the VIP room?"

Our *Walpurgisnacht* was not going to end so soon, as Sam insisted we all accompany him. I was reminded of the U.N., which often sends so-called "observers," who sit by impotently as the local population is slaughtered by the latest self styled "liberation movement."

Sam disputed my characterization of sex as an intellectual activity.

"Everything is subjective, intellectual or not, but *intellectual* implies the Sisyphean attempt at ratiocination, and sexuality is a succumbing to man's animal nature. Once I let go of the slim tethers that tie me to so-called reality and I'm in that VIP room, I'll be preconscious. That is to say, I'll be at the mercy of both the primitive demiurge and hallucinatory ecstasies. So therefore I'm urging the two of you to accompany me so I don't end up doing something foolish. Anyway, for scientific, sociological, and historical reasons, I'd like you to document my descent or ascent—whichever way you choose to describe turning over reason to instinct. Schopenhauer said that reason was the only way we could resist the demands of the will. I disagree. There is no way. But let's see."

We followed Sam as the black dancer said, "Okay, honey." Her frame was narrow for the explosive sensuality of her buttocks and her large breasts, and her back was totally smooth and unmarked. In fact, the skin had a curiously lighter color that made it look like she was covered by some large white birthmark from her coccyx to the nape of her neck.

Her name was Giselle. Her mother had been Haitian and her father German—the son of a convicted officer at Treblinka who was still held in high esteem amongst right-wing German politicians. Sam was more interested in having her pose than in engaging in any of the offerings—fellatio at $150, fuck $250, with $275 buying "around the world." Bill said he had some questions to ask about her past. That, Giselle replied, would be $100 for a half an hour. Bill asked Giselle to assume the doggy sex position with her ass raised high in the air. Giselle lowered herself down to the carpeted floor of the VIP room and we pulled up chairs behind her. She'd been an architecture student in Düsseldorf, but had dropped out to study dance and then classic French theater in Paris. She had studied at the Comédie-Française and had gotten so far as being an understudy for one of the supernumeraries in a production of Corneille's *Le Cid*, but the esthetic rewards of the classical stage didn't justify the near-poverty conditions. She was happier as a lap dancer in Key West.

"I feel I'm helping people," she said. She had the flexibility of a yogi and talked confidently despite what might have been an awkward posture for others.

At Bill's urging, Giselle recited a short scene from *Le Cid* on all fours. As she spoke Corneille's words, she stared back at us. The recitation stimulated a discussion of Levi-Strauss' *The Raw and the Cooked*, which continued on as we were walking out of the VIP room.

I was starting to feel pangs. Now that I'd actually been separated from *her* and there was no chance that we could scan presences like bats in the night, my ability to conceive of her in my imagination was taking precedence over my animal side. I noticed I was going through a dramatic internal change in which I was beginning to think of her as a person instead of feeling a purely instinctual desire for an object I didn't even want to know. Our mating pattern was broken. Having short circuited the instinctual way we found each other, I began to worry about how and when I would ever be able to see her again. I was homesick. I missed her cunt, I missed my regular fuckings, I felt guilty for leaving and fearful of retribution. After all, I wouldn't have liked her pulling her cunt out from under me unexpectedly. No one likes a dick that takes a walk. I had no telephone numbers, no addresses. I couldn't call, e-mail, or send post cards. In fact, getting in touch with her at all was totally impossible since I didn't even know her name. Not only did I miss her cunt, the truth was I missed her. I missed her even though I couldn't remember her face or anything about her. I even missed the inane remarks she made when she was trying unsuccessfully to create an air of normality after sex. I didn't love her. I'd never loved anybody except my mother, though I was becoming increasingly fond of Bill, who had also become a mother figure to me. But two things were obvious: I was experiencing separation anxiety and an almost supernatural level of horniness. Neither Giselle nor the sex club had anything to do with the latter, but the fact is, even a short break seems like an eternity when you've been fucking two or three times a night.

I didn't want to alarm Bill or Sam, nor did I want to ruin their good time, but I was a loose cannon. I considered my options. I could hop on a plane, but I didn't know what awaited me on the other side; surely there'd be no welcoming party at the airport. I could try to find a hooker in Key West. But going to a hooker, for someone who has experienced weeks of mutually explosive sexuality with his partner, is like eating a Big Mac in the middle of Paris. You can get one, but does it satisfy an eroticism so intense it eradicates the boundary lines of personality? It is very difficult to communicate the noumenal essence of such ecstasy. I'm sure Kant himself would have had a hard time.

We'd passed a Zen meditation center on our way to the lap dancing place. Once I got on the bench, I would at least be able to cool down. I told Bill that I had an upset stomach. I'd meet the two of them back at the hotel. I was sure Bill was going to offer to get Sam to drive me (in which case I'd have to go overboard, insisting I wouldn't do anything to ruin their night), but no excuses were necessary. They were too busy ogling a whole new slew of dancers. There wasn't a peep out of either of them when I said, "I'll just grab a cab out front."

I arrived in the middle of a meditation that appeared to be attended almost exclusively by sex workers. Every bench was taken up by babes whose relaxed state didn't prevent their hardened nipples from poking out of their tank tops. The *oms* brought back the memory of an amazing hum job my high school girlfriend gave me. I remember it well because it occurred the same afternoon we learned Kennedy had been assassinated. We'd skipped out of school between classes so we could get to her house before her mother got home from her job as a school crossing guard. Her mother found us sneaking back into the school building. From the look on her face, I thought we were in deep trouble, but it was she who told us what had happened to the president. That was actually the beginning of my long and harrowing struggle with impotence. I was already burdened with fear about my father's jealousy of my mother and me, and on top of that I'd been having sex during a national tragedy. From then on, every time I went to bed with a woman, I worried.

My meditation was troubled. At first it was the usual long road leading to a dazzling white light, but then the light began to flutter the way a bulb does when it's not screwed in properly or the filament is about to burn out. I was immersed in a dark forest. Hot winds that smelled like perfumed fish buffeted me back and forth. I realized that I was like the character in the Almodovar film, *Talk to Her* (2002), a latter-day Gulliver negotiating his way in a Brobdingnagian-sized pussy (and by the way, I was a total film buff until my obsession with her came along, replacing the celluloid). The dark bushes and thick growths I was trudging through were her pubic hair. I started to sweat. I wanted to open my eyes, to get out of it, but I'm compulsive when it comes to meditating. No matter what transpires, no matter how upsetting the thoughts, I always try to walk through the feelings. Now I felt I was suffocating. In reality she suffered from cunt fart, and in the meditation her farting cunt was throwing me to the ground and taking the wind out of me. I kept waiting for the sound of the timer that would indicate the meditation was over. I'd come late for the class and the actual meditation wasn't supposed to last more than twenty minutes, but I felt as if I'd been sitting there for hours. I can easily sit on a meditation bench in a *seiza* position, but now my legs were cramping. I felt claustrophobic. I didn't think I could take one more minute when the little alarm started to beep. "Okay," the leader said, "now I'm going to bring you back."

The lights went on; the candles and incense were both snuffed out. A few of the babes went to the bathroom. I don't always stay for the discussion session at these things, but I needed to talk. I was the first to raise my hand.

"I know there are a lot of women here, but I have to be honest. In my meditation today I got lost in my girlfriend's pussy." There was a loud guffaw from the back of the room. I ignored it. "I can't even remember her face, though even now I'm inundated with olfactory reminiscences. I feel like a blind man. She is all around me. I feel her, I smell her, I can taste her in my mouth, but I can't find her. I never have found her, but it hasn't bothered me until this moment when we are actually separated by space and time. My meditation caused added anxiety because I've been retroactively suffering from the degree to which I never even knew her when I was with her. Our separation has made me acutely aware of my denial in this area. All in all, it was a good meditation because it made me feel these things. I'm not dissatisfied. Sometimes meditation is supposed to bring up painful emotions." By the time I was finished, almost all the women had left the room.

I was going to apologize to the leader for causing the exodus, but a wave of indignation swept over me. I hadn't done anything wrong. I didn't deserve to be punished. If anything, it was they who were being rude. Hadn't I already suffered enough? Amidst all the pain, I came to the realization of how important her pussy was to me. I had denigrated our... I still didn't know what to call it—love? passion? physical interactiveness?—because it didn't fit into the traditional structures of white male dominated Western love. Books like Denis de Rougemont's *Love in the Western World*, which I'd read in college, had had a deleterious effect on my imagination, creating a feeling that love was X, sex was Y. The categories made me think that the thing we call love should work from the head down, when in my case it was working from the crotch up. Yes, I was in love with a vagina, a vulva, even a uterus, but it didn't mean I couldn't love a mind, nor did it mean that I should, though in all likelihood I would. The memory of the salty smell of her pussy would be the inspiration that'd make her the Gretchen of my latter-day Faust tale. We had transcended our selves through the ecstasy of our great fucks, but we would also experience a spiritual transcendence in which we'd rediscover them. Inevitably, we would find the true essence of each other's beings.

I got a cab and headed back to the hotel. The cab driver, an elderly black man, had one of those beaten up '60s radios, where you pushed the black buttons to get the station. I hadn't heard such muted music since I was a teenager, and the contrast was all the more dramatic since he was tuned into the local hip-hop station, which plainly required a more contemporary form of amplification. I looked over at the odometer and I saw the car had more than 500,000 miles on it. That cab had been to the equivalent of the moon and back. It was a black Ford Fairlane whose chrome had rusted off. The hip-hop version of "I Got a Woman" was playing and it made me want to cry. I was hot, my legs itched, and I missed her two hair-covered lips more than I had ever missed anything before. It was as if those lips were talking to me and saying *I want to end the relationship*, a projection that only increased the excitement that was building inside of me.

Most of the great revelations of my life have come to me when I'm standing on my head. I can stand anywhere, but when I do it for an extended period, I find a wall to lean my legs against; that way my legs remain absolutely straight. I removed the oil painting of Key West Harbor from the wall of our hotel room, cupped my hands around my head, and started raising myself up. It's at times like this that I'm grateful for my years of yoga. The only problem was, by now I had a hard-on. I looked like one of those totem poles where the carvings of the warrior gods jut out of the wood. My dick was so stiff I began to worry: If the phone rang or the fire alarm went off, I might fall on it and damage myself. I needed to free myself from the priapic state of mind to which I'd become enslaved. I gradually lowered myself to the ground. The dreaded scourge of impotence which I'd loathed and feared, the way the people of the Middle Ages feared the plague, didn't seem like the end of the world anymore. The hated loss of erection that had so troubled my adolescence in the aftermath of the Kennedy assassination, the thing I'd run away from for years, in fact, now seemed appealing. When you walk around with a baseball bat in your pants, you live in perpetual fear of hurting either yourself or others.

I'm one of those people who has always gotten hard-ons in the wrong place at the wrong time—for example, in subways and buses and while standing in front of a room full of undergraduates when I was a teaching assistant. Finally I found a way to handle the situation. Like a lot of discoveries in the history of science, it came about by accident. I was on my way to the Museum of Jewish Heritage—A Living Memorial to the

Holocaust in Manhattan—with an erection that wouldn't go away. Stopping to take a piss didn't help matters; no sooner had I urinated than it popped up all over again. It was a particularly busy day for me. I have pyorrhea, and after the museum I had to get to my gum specialist. After that, I had an appointment with a Broadway producer. I kept trying to cover up my appendage by pulling my raincoat over it, which made me look even more suspicious. I was not only tired, but embarrassed. Then, magically, when I walked into the memorial and saw the images of the suffering in the camps, lo and behold, my erection went away. Ever since then, thinking about concentration camps has provided relief. It's not a long-term solution to the problem. The minute my mind wanders, my dick pops back up. If I keep reminding myself to think *Dachau, Bergen-Belsen, Thierenstadt,* I'm in business.

This cooling down process allowed me to return to standing on my head. I stood on my head with images of emaciated concentration camp victims running through my mind. I thought of the piles of glasses, human hair, and gold extracted from teeth before I slowly rolled out of my headstand in order to pick up the ringing phone. It was a woman's voice.

"Hi." For a moment I froze. It was familiar. I felt a tingle down my spine. I couldn't place the voice, yet I felt it was someone I'd always known.

"I'm looking for Bill." I couldn't believe it. I was ecstatic and terrified at the same time.

"Is this you?"

"As far as I know I haven't left my body."

"It's me."

"Well I hope so. You see, that's the nature of syntax. You are you, and I am I. This is something we can agree on. Beyond this we plunge into the depths of subjectivity. I studied with Hilary Putnam at Harvard, but I still haven't been able to breach the idealist chasm. How do I know you exist? I don't, but I can answer your initial question proudly. *Yes, this is me.*"

"Maybe it isn't you after all. For a minute I thought it was."

"Well thanks, buster. Nothing like someone doubting your existence for you. Helluva way to wrap up my day."

"Sorry, I just thought you were someone else?" Whew, close call. I was dripping with sweat and my hard-on had returned. When I'd gone through my periodic bouts of impotence as a teenager, I'd tried to think up sexy scenarios to get myself going, but I'd be so nervous I couldn't even think, and when I could, I found I wasn't turned on by the things that normally, effortlessly did the trick. I'd think *breast* or *cunt*, and the idea would occur to me they were no different from any other part of the anatomy. Pubic hair was just hair. A breast was just flesh. Vaginas were folded flesh. So what? Now I had the same problem in trying to get rid of my hard-on. Thinking of piles of emaciated corpses didn't do the trick. I was too aware I was thinking horrible thoughts to get rid of my hard-on. Self-consciousness overruled substance and I wasn't able to do anything about the hot throbbing hard-on bursting against my fly.

When I was a teenager, I was a constant victim of passionate and unreciprocated love. Everywhere I went, I thought I was seeing someone I had a crush on. My romanticism was aggravated by the impotence problem. It was safer to run after women I couldn't have. Eventually something had to give. My sexual life was a little like Germany after the Versailles treaty. My pride and my manhood had both been crushed—in this case by my own sensitive nature. My attempt to compensate for the constant feelings of defeat turned me into the satyr I'd become. I made myself over in the spirit of those advertisements in the old men's magazines where the hundred-pound weakling becomes a total stud. Legendary womanizers like Pushkin and Hugo, the mystery writer George Simenon, who always fucked the chambermaids in the hotels he stayed in (amongst numerous other daily trysts), and Wilt Chamberlain, who had 10,000 conquests amidst his thousands of baskets, all became role models for me. I studied Henry Miller and Frank Harris and eradicated Goethe's *Sufferings of Young Werther* and Rilke's *Letters to a Young Poet* from my memory. I became a tough guy, an ass man. I hung out at a boxing gym. I learned to treat women like objects. I realized my father was never going to come after me; he didn't have the guts since I'd grown bigger and stronger from all my working out. I found myself with the equivalent of a new set of wheels and chassis. The libido is a constant stream whose flow is only interrupted by mind. I was flooded with libidinous energy that had always existed in me, but which my psychohistory had never allowed me to experience before.

But now I was thrown back to my youthful romantic years when I'd been haunted by fleeting images of lost loves. I was flooded with the sensation of my hot throbbing cock pushing through thick bush to get to a pussy whose wetness and hotness, whose facility for invagination was unparalleled in my experience—a pussy that kept receding before me.

All spiritual seekers from Augustine onwards live in a certain blindness that requires faith. I didn't know what I would face when I went home. *Could you have imagined the whole fucking thing? If you've been porking a bitch whose face you don't remember, something's wrong. You don't remember how you found yourselves in each others arms? C'mon!* I couldn't stop the thoughts. Worse than finding she was tired of me, didn't want me, or didn't want to keep cheating on her boyfriend was the possibility that the fucking hadn't happened at all. Remember the girl in Hitchcock's *Vertigo* (1958)? She doesn't exist. The James Stewart character's fallen in love with a chimera. It's a passion predicated on impossibility. The haunting quality of the Stewart character's love is its unreality. I'm a Shakespeare buff and I'd read an essay comparing *Vertigo* to late Shakespeare plays like *The Winter's Tale*, where imagination triumphs over reality and the dead are brought back to life. Was I chasing a phantom pussy?

Now my desire to know was overcoming my fear. If there were only some way I could call her. Intelligence services had all kinds of methods of identifying people. She didn't need me to be a hot pussy. Her pussy was independently hot, which meant she'd undoubtedly had plenty of guys before me. I've known many women married to someone who provides stability and what, for a hot woman, is essentially Platonic love. These kinds of women fuck their husbands once a week for the sake of appearance and satisfy their real sexuality elsewhere. She had to have left a trail of previous lovers, who were undoubtedly already occupying the empty space in her bed (a thought that added jealousy to my already overwrought condition). She was a member of the sexual aristocracy—a group of men and women with inordinate sexual needs and the kind of superhuman physiological capacities necessary to satisfy them. The government must be keeping track of them to make sure they never went to work for the CIA. You put a highly sexualized person in a sensitive security situation, and you run the risk of leaks. I called information and asked for the number of the CIA campus, but when the automated operator said, *Verizon is now connecting your call to*, I hung up.

There was only one other solution—hypnosis. If I couldn't find her once I was back home, I could go back in my memory to our first fuck; I could figure out when and where we met, and from there I'd be able to figure out how I knew her. One thing would lead to the next. A butcher, a baker—any local storekeeper might provide the clue. All I needed was one person who knew her and understood my problem—someone who could lean over the counter and whisper to her, "There's somebody desperately trying to get in touch with you."

Did she have a picture of me in her mind, or was I only a dick, just as she was a cunt? Did she have as little idea of my face as I had of hers? Finding the face to match the cunt I was looking for would be like finding a needle in a haystack. I kept thinking *my life is over*. My erection kept coming back. My longing for her cunt would eventually kill me. I could see my obit in the paper: *died of complications from priapism*. A sustained erection can do to the penis what diabetes does to the extremities—render it painful, useless, and in need of amputation.

The thing I feared most was in danger of coming true. I'd always been afraid of retribution. Pleasure wouldn't go unpunished. When I'd set out to invent my new self, to create a macho personality, I'd read a hundred self-help books that told me it was neurotic to worry. I'd finally caved in to all the analysts, therapists, healers, and assorted gurus who argued there was nothing to be afraid of. Now it turned out I'd been right in the first place. The best place for my dick was squished up against my balls like a fig; letting it hang out, sticking it out proudly in the world, would result in little more than it getting lopped off.

I left a note for Bill and his friend, Sam, and took off for the airport, even though it meant I was going to have to pay my own way. I made a list for Bill. When he got back, I wanted to try the meatloaf and mashed potatoes he was always bragging about. Bill dabbled in such styles as *cuisine classique* and *cuisine minceur* since he couldn't stand repeating the same specialties all the time, but he basically believed in classic American dishes like meatloaf, apple pie, mashed potatoes, corn fritters, and fried chicken. He was a deconstructionist as far as food was concerned because, as he explained, "Nothing dramatizes as much as food, how culture-bound our assumptions are." It might be hard to argue that some neighborhood rapper was as great as Shakespeare, but when it came to food, who was I to say that *coquilles St. Jacques* or *lobster thermidor* were superior to a cheese burger? However, I could say without a doubt that our lovemaking was superior to anything that I or perhaps anyone on earth had ever experienced, and that her pussy was one of the finest sexual specimens in the world.

I was suffering from the blindness of passion. The emotion I felt towards her was so powerful I couldn't even remember who she was. Yet like the blind man who compensates for his condition with increasing acuity in his other sensory faculties, I had built up a sixth sense in so far as the inside of her vagina was concerned. No matter how wet and hot another woman's cunt was, no matter how powerfully a woman was able to draw my prick in with her vaginal muscle, there was no way I could be fooled. I would have known her cunt anywhere. If I suffered a form of agnosia in which I couldn't recognize the face of the person for whom I felt sexual passion, I had made up for it with an archeologist-level appreciation for the walls of the cunt. My prick had scoured the crevices, the surfaces, it had plummeted, it had rolled, it had inspected, it had unleashed, it had crawled, it had plowed, it had prodded. No gynecologist examining her in stirrups contained my knowledge, because in the end it wasn't only a knowledge of hair follicles, skin, veins, muscles, emissions, viscosity, temperature (after all she wasn't an engine whose exhaust was being examined for an annual motor vehicle inspection), it was all these physical things rolled up into a ball. Porn movies give the impression that sex is simply a matter of equipment. To extend the automotive metaphor, it's as if sex were simply a matter of finding the right driver for the car, the right saddle or jockey for the horse. But she and I were more than a stiff prick and a lubricious cunt (though these phenomenological elements didn't hurt). The powerful emotions that derived from our sexual congress, the elements that in fact optimized the effectiveness of my cock and her pussy, were composed of the ineffable mixture of unconscious desires and affects that create the mystery of attraction, the fuel for the engine, as it were—even when only the genitals were involved.

More than once on the way to the airport I told the cab driver, a longhaired kid who kept playing Bob Dylan's "Lay Lady Lay" over and over again on his CD player, to hit the brakes. I kept thinking I was seeing her, even though I couldn't activate the memory chip that would have given away the secret of her identity. I still didn't know what the hell she looked like. I felt like one of those Kennedy assassination freaks who play and replay the Zabruder film (1963), trying to discover something that wasn't there. The fact is when you don't know who someone is, almost anyone can be them, and in fact just about anyone who remotely fills the bill becomes a candidate. I screamed so loudly for the cab driver to stop at one point that he stopped short, causing the car in back of us to hit our fender. I didn't have time for insurance companies and the police and immediately offered each of the offended parties $50 bills. The last time I screamed out, I told the cab driver to pull over. I was sure it was her. My candidate turned out to be a twenty-one-year-old Hispanic hooker named Hilda, who when I asked, "Are you her?" offered to be anything I wanted her to be and change into any outfit I wanted so that she could be it, at the price of $100 for a half-hour session or enough drugs to satisfy her "crank" habit. That's Key West for you; in that kind of heat, women don't think twice about taking off their clothes.

Hilda and I walked from Ocean Avenue to the infamous Duval Street, where the mixture of working girls, guys, and chicken hawks reminded me of the Tenderloin in San Francisco. She wasn't wearing panties, so when she pulled up her dress, I was able to see she wasn't my passion; she shaved. A lot of your common street hookers these days are either graduates of creative writing programs in top universities who regard prostitution as research for the novel, play, or collection of short stories they're working on, or they're addicts. Hilda was actually a combination of both. There's been a rash of this life-and-art confusion with Ivy League-educated girls becoming wrestlers, garbage collectors, and in one case even a professional boxer who ended up with an 8-9 record before selling her first novel, *Rubber Gloves*. During the course of trying to entice me by playing with her clit, Hilda started discussing Rilke's *Letters to a Young Poet* with me. We'd both read it as high school students in the original Schocken edition and had both taken great solace in the cover design. Since we had established a good rapport, I asked her if she would mind if I stuck my finger in her pussy just to confirm she wasn't my lost love. I even offered to pay extra, but she wouldn't hear of it. My finger slid right in, and I have to say there were some striking similarities, especially with regard to the topography of the inner walls. I hadn't reached my destination, but I was on the right track!

I liked Hilda and our brief meeting inaugurated a correspondence about German literature that would go on for years, but that's another story.

I got to the airport, but my hard-on was becoming increasingly unwieldy. It bumped against my luggage as I was getting out of the cab, and I was already having trouble as I waited on line to be ticketed. We were told to keep the line moving. When I did so, my prick poked into the back of a young woman with short blond hair who was continually yelling at her two children to "be still." When she turned around, looking for one of the kids to slap, she saw the tent poking of out of my pants. For a moment I was terrified. What would she do? Some situations simply defy responses. It would have been embarrassing to me if she'd yelled out in her thick Southern drawl, "Hey y'all, this guy gotta hard-on," but it would have been even more embarrassing for her. Some real perpetrators (which I wasn't) must have been spared conviction by women who couldn't get words like "dick," "prick," "hard-on," or "erection" out of their mouths. She just scoffed and turned away. A minute later I saw her land one right against the cheek of a small child, who burst into tears as she screamed, "Where the hell have y'all been?"

What was I going to do in the close quarters of the plane? How would I get down the aisle without my erection crashing into the person in front of me? How would I hide my rock-hard prick? And what would happen if I couldn't get rid of my erection? Any erection that exceeds four hours is a real danger to its owner. Sometimes ice works, but if it's untreated with phylephrine or decongestants like terbutalin, the tissue can actually become necrotic. I'd heard of a guy who shot himself up with one of those impotence drugs and had an erection for five days. He ended up with a one-inch prick. The first sign is discomfort. My prick hadn't begun to ache, but what if it did? I wasn't worried about the first leg of my journey, a small hop over to Miami. It was my connecting flight that I was concerned about. Would I be able to tell the pilot to turn back if the Holocaust imagery and ice packs didn't help to get the erection to go down?

While I was waiting on line, I had one more experience that to this day makes me question the relationship between the phenomenal and noumenal worlds. I was edging closer up to the ticket counter. There was only one agent working the flight to Miami and it was a long serpentine line. I couldn't stop thinking about Hilda's cunt (despite it's dissimilarity to that of my beloved) and how welcomed my finger felt inside of her, though her deadened doper's eyes gave no hint of her excitement. And I couldn't get rid of my hard-on. There was a couple doing the next best thing to getting divorced right in front of me. Not only were they calling each other names, they were loudly splitting up the property. "You take the fucking house, I'll take the Jag."

"You take the brats, but I get Fidel." Finally the husband threw her plane ticket to the floor and stormed off with his in hand.

She was the kind of woman who models her appearance on a Barbie Doll. She used a lot of pancake makeup, wore her platinum blond hair in a wavy permanent, and sported a short pleated skirt. Right away I knew it was her. I smelt the aroma of our sex. Well, push came to shove, and as I moved ahead and she stepped back and bent over to pick up the tickets, I was sure that she wasn't wearing panties and that I had penetrated her in spite of and right through my pants. I wasn't surprised. If it was her (and there was reason to believe it was, considering how unhappy she was in her relationship, whose status, i.e. marriage, for all I knew, she had been lying about), then the close proximity could have resulted in copulation. I looked down at my crotch and noticed a stain that could have been caused by her lubricity if what I thought had occurred had indeed occurred. But before I could inquire, she was gone. I noticed her screaming at her husband and banging his chest with her fists after we'd gone through security.

☙

Before I'd met *her*—years after my sexual problems had given way to promiscuity—I'd gone through a period when I'd actually become bored by sex. Due to the circumstances of my life, I'd had a number of women who were allowing me to have my way with them, and the very availability of the thing I had always desired created its own ennui. I felt like a dessert-lover confronted with a sickeningly large smorgasbord of the most tempting napoleons, éclairs, soufflés, parfaits, crème brûlés, tartes tatins, and chocolate mousses. I'd attended several orgies in Paris when I was sent over to consult on the sets for a French version of *West Side Story*. There was a prominent French art critic who'd succeeded in getting herself gangbanged over and over again for the sake of a book she was writing. I participated in several of these bacchanals, which generally occurred in the parking lot of the Beaubourg, but I found myself yawning during these events, and on one embarrassing occasion even fell asleep inside of her. I was facing a crisis. If nothing interested me, if even the most perverse sexual scenarios lost their allure, what was there to live for? Then I met her. It was as if I'd been given an elixir. All at once, I was filled with the same cravings I'd felt in all the years when anonymous sex was the utopia I dreamt of—except they were focused on one person. I had to find her, or I would fall back into the world of humdrum promiscuity.

As the stewardess bent down to serve me my Diet Coke, I was so hard I felt my prick almost touch her tits. There is a certain kind of woman who can detect true sexual energy the way a strong magnet will pick up stray tacks, pins, and nails. And when she looked at me I knew she was thinking about my hard cock running between those two tits. Tit fucking had been a part of our lovemaking, as was rimming. I needed to get off that plane. I had to get to her! I went to the bathroom five times to ice my prick. I started to repeat the mantra from the meditation class: *segi, sabi, subi*. Again and again I mumbled the words. I had to calm myself down or people would start to get suspicious about my agitation and think I was a terrorist. In fact, during one of my excursions to the bathroom, the plane experienced some turbulence and my dick shot into the back of another stewardess who, the way she cried out, must have mistaken my hard-on for the barrel of a gun. I apologized profusely, blaming her trauma on a magic marker which I said was "sticking the wrong way in my pocket." It made no sense, but as everyone knows, in spite of all the terrorism in the world, security on planes is still not what it should be.

The ice finally did the job and I relaxed and enjoyed the

flight. However, the minute the landing gear descended and the prospect of being reunited became a real possibility, I was in trouble again. I was like one of those pigeons Marlon Brando raised in *On the Waterfront* (1954). But this pigeon wasn't looking for another home; it was looking for a cunt that had the perfection of Eva-Marie Saint's face. My six-inch hard-on extended out in front of me, its mass hurling me towards objects more quickly than usual. So the electric eye that operated in and out of the baggage pickup, which would have been programmed to open when a traveler came within three feet of the entrance, opened for me a good nine feet in advance of the rest of my body.

As soon as I entered the arrivals terminal, I heard my name over the public address system. It turned out to be Bill, on the phone.

"How the hell did you know I was here?"

"I have to tell you I love you. I've always loved you. From the moment I laid eyes on you, I wanted to suck your cock."

I was so flabbergasted the only thing I could say was, "We've only known each other for three weeks."

"Thinking about your big hard cock has been my *raison d'etre*. That bus station's Jeffrey Dahmer territory. Many of the guys who pick up homeless men are sadists. I was nuts to go off with you. I just couldn't control myself."

"But what about the lap dancing club, the wife and the kid?"

"The wife and kid were classic defenses. I was covering up my gay side; all the male bonding about pussy and gangbangs functioned the same way—as camouflages for homoerotic drives."

"But I didn't notice you acting with the disgust most fags have towards tits and cunts."

"Why do you think we were talking about Foucault? Keeping a deconstructionist French queer in the conversation was akin to having a life raft. Personally, when I see pussy, which isn't often, I feel like I'm drowning. I start to gag. I can't breathe."

I realized there and then that all my problems would be solved if I could only become gay, a distinct possibility since I have nothing against cocks, but the idea that I might ever be disgusted by the thing that was such an ongoing source of pleasure and torment was a risk I wasn't ready to take.

"I don't love you, Bill. You're a great cook and a nice guy, but I hope you're not hanging on to the notion you'll be dining on my prick."

"Can we talk about this? I was sure you were closet the minute I laid eyes on you, and I have a great track record. All these obsessions with her are either a fantasy or a massive defense over the—to you—horrifying notion you're gay."

I could have let my mind go in the direction Bill was talking about. I could have bought the gay S&M magazines with the big black inmates who'd easily propose marriage to a fellow like me. But I didn't want to be anyone's wife. Not yet. I wasn't ready for such a paradigm shift. Hot cunt was the foundation of my universe, and hers in particular was my world. Addicts won't give up their addictions if they don't get the idea that what they think is pleasure is really a form of pain. I was still at the stage where I didn't care what it was called. I had to have the thing that kept my dick as hard as a rock—even when the rock-hardness, which could come on me at any hour of the day and night, might hurt and even be damaging to my prick's vascular structure.

A radical and revolutionary change in my definition of pleasure, which would affirm the self while allowing for the kind of selfless transcendence I'd been experiencing, was what was required, but not before I fucked her at least one more time. The usual romantic jargon *I need to hold you in my arms* was meaningless. I had never held her in my arms. Generally my arms were locked on the bed posts, which I used to launch ever more powerful thrusts of a dick that could have freed itself from the gravitational pull of the earth if its energies had not been diverted. My dick would have made Werner von Braun proud.

I told Bill I had to go, even though I didn't know where the hell I was going, but not before reminding him about the meatloaf he'd promised to make me.

"Just because I want you to get your mind off my meat doesn't mean you have to forget the beef."

"I feel sad."

"Bill, I really like you—as a friend." Even as I was talking, my eyes were scouring the airport parking lot. You never could tell. I might easily hone in on her like a heat-seeking missile. Reason was thrown out the door when it came to her pussy, and weird things happened in the fever of passion—things that defeated all rational explanation. Yes, I didn't know what she looked like, where she lived, or anything about her, but I would find her. She could be in the white 1972 Lincoln Continental pulling out of the space marked A4104, just as she could be the slender stewardess in Midwest Air uniform, walking smartly through the main lobby pulling her carry-on behind her.

છ

I couldn't imagine her appearance, as hard as I tried, but when I spotted her as I came out of my favorite pizzeria, I knew—this time with real surety—it was *her*. I knew her the way a dog knows his master. You know how dogs start barking even before anyone is in sight or even in smelling distance? I just sensed it was her. I have to admit I was a bit disappointed. I like fleshy women with big firm tits and large aureoles, the kind of women who don't need to go to the gym five days a week to have a perfectly rounded ass. She had a boyish frame and short cropped hair. She actually looked like one of those Shakespearean characters, a woman who looks enough like a man to disguise herself as one. For the first time I forced myself to think before we engaged with each other. I made a mental note *remember what she looks like.* I started to follow her, and when I was only a few steps behind, she spun around, unzipped my fly, pushing me at the same time into the vestibule of her building. Before I had a chance to get a word out, she had my dick in her mouth.

We had a lot to catch up on and we were doing it in our usual wordless way. I could tell she had noticed I was gone by the vehemence of her attack. I had generally had enough control of my senses to tease her hole before going in for the kill. But before I had a chance to use the ratiocinative elements of my lovemaking capacity, she had her finger jammed up my asshole. I was reminded of that climactic scene of a children's movie called *Old Grizzly* (1955), when the mother bear spots her missing cubs at the bottom of a steep, winding trail and barrels down, a huge top-heavy presence on a steep trail, in defiance of the laws of gravity. I was yelling like a cowboy subduing a bucking bronco in the rodeo. However, in my case, none of it was for the audience. I was too out of myself to have any awareness of my actual performance. At one point in our lovemaking I remember thinking *you've got to stop, you have to put an end to this, to talk to her instead of fucking every minute.* Yet once it started, there wasn't anything that could hold us back, and afterwards I found myself wandering the neighborhood, happily satiated, proud of my prowess as usual, and suffering from the same amnesia for what had transpired between us as I had so many times before.

We had fucked so hard, and were so spent when it was over, that I never got a chance to ask if she would leave her boyfriend for me. It wasn't even a question. We were like marathon runners. Both of us lay on the bed totally exhausted. Being a male, I was actually like a shot putter in the Olympics after all that thrusting. But what would have happened if I'd asked her? I'd have been vulnerable. Would she have regarded me as too dependent and needy? Would our chemistry have been lost once I expressed the intensity of my feelings for her? Even if it was true, how could I say she meant so much to me when I never really knew her? I felt hampered by a history, by a past that gave me the exultation I felt and prevented me from attaining the stability and predictability I yearned for.

I had some big decisions to make. Every time I walked out of her apartment, I departed without any guarantee I would see her again. I had no way of getting assurances. My passion was all based on faith. I never knew what would happen next. Wouldn't it be better to have transcendental sex plus the security of an ongoing relationship, where she, not Bill, was cooking my beef? But if I tried to make things different, I might destroy everything.

I was getting myself into a state of hysteria. I arrived home to find that Bill had sacrificed his business-fare ticket and hopped the next plane. He'd made me a surprise meatloaf dinner. I went on and on about how wonderful it was, how surprised I was, how special the smell was, but I had no appetite. How could I? I didn't even know what time it was or what day of the week. I forced myself to eat, all the while having to pretend I didn't notice Bill's eyes fixated on the perpetual bulge in my crotch. Eating that meatloaf was like a brutal workout, like doing wind sprints and pushups in 100-degree heat. I had to force my mouth to chew—all the while using up energy with my torment. What should I do? Yes, I would fuck her once more, but what about the time after that? If I brought up the question of having a real relationship, she might bolt and I would never see her again. I belched loudly. Bill's eyes were filled with infinite compassion, the infinite compassion of a gay Buddha who'd turned rough trade in bus terminal bathrooms.

It's a good thing I'm a set designer because the off-again,

on-again nature of the work allowed me to carry on an intense relationship in the beginning. When I'm out of work, as I was then, I have loads of time. Following my return from Key West, my schedule was more complicated, yet still manageable. I'd be flown out to Duluth or Boise for a day's work on shows that were already running and return home in time to find my dick as deeply embedded in the soft wet folds of her pussy as the engravings are on the sarcophagus of an Egyptian empress. But a busy period followed. I had to mount *My Fair Lady* in Columbus and *Annie* in Green Bay and after that *West Side Story* in Austin. The more I was called away for shows, the fewer chances there were for these occurrences. I was so desperate that I thought seriously of canceling some of my gigs, but then lost my nerve. People who do what I do are a dime a dozen. If I stopped showing up, I'd get the kind of reputation I didn't need. On the other hand, my old Tourette's was beginning to surface—primarily because I wasn't getting pussy. I'd call out "mommy" when I was trying to make a point to the director of a show. I screamed out "I wanna fuck" as an Annie in Burlington, Vermont, crooned "Tomorrow."

"Seek and you shall find," Bill said on my return home from one of these outings.

"What's fir dinna?"

"Your favorite."

"Not meatloaf."

"And you don't have to ask, of course mashed potatoes." I had fucked her the minute I'd gotten back, and I'd forgotten to eat. I didn't realize how hungry I was. I chopped off huge pieces of the meatloaf, submerging them in Bill's creamy mashed potatoes, but I was so hungry that I couldn't really appreciate the parsley, the sage, the cumin, the subtleties of the curry-like seasoning that makes Bill's meatloaf so special. Don't get me wrong, it's your classic American meatloaf rounded at the top with a twist of ketchup, but Bill always puts a little extra zing into it that's akin to finding an actually useful saying inside a fortune cookie. I realized another thing as I was wolfing down the food. I was so horny by the time I saw her after these trips that I was not enjoying most of the fine points of the fucking the way I had in the days before this busy spell. I was like a hunter with a ten-gauge shotgun in the middle of deer season. I was just looking for my target. I was so worked up by the time we got together that I could do little more than thrust my dick right into her hot hole. There was none of the touching, the buildup, that tantalizing foreplay, where I'd suck on her nipples as she stuck her finger up my ass, that occurred on the days we saw each other before these trips. I missed tugging her dingleberries in the heat of passion. It had been a long time since she stuck her nails in my back and drew blood as she sunk her teeth into my lips. Not only that, I never knew if she would be waiting.

I had to do something, but I felt paralyzed by inertia. It was the paradox of my condition that I could be made so passive by the explosiveness of our sexuality. I started to rehearse in my head what I would say to her. *I know*, I would say about her boyfriend, *that you have been with him for a long time, and I know that you've had a satisfying relationship, or you wouldn't be with him. I don't know him and he doesn't know me. However, I have the distinct feeling that I have something to offer that he doesn't.* Now that was succinct and to the point. I wasn't grandstanding. I wasn't allowing myself preposterous Wagnerian protestations of love. I wasn't saying anything that was going to make her nervous. I was calling a spade a spade. Volcanic fucking. That's what I had to offer that her boyfriend didn't. Then I went on to rehearse how I was going to stop myself from jumping right in the sack the minute she unzipped my fly. Would I grab her by the wrist for instance? That seemed too remonstrative. I had to practice restraint. I used some of the imaging techniques I'd learned in therapy years before when I was trying to reshape my libido. I visualized her holding my penis in her hand, even putting it in her mouth. I visualized holding her gently as I intoned the magic words *I want a committed relationship*. No, not *I want a committed relationship*; *I want a committed relationship with you, I want to commit myself to you. I love you*. No. I couldn't tell her I loved her; I didn't know her well enough. But love was something I imagined coming out of the increased commitment we would be making to each other.

Then there were other questions. Did I want the boyfriend to move out so I could move in? Did I want the boyfriend to move out so I could simply be alone with her after we fucked? Did I want a trial period in which he moved out, but still remained in her life, so she could weigh the two of us side by side and decide what she wanted? I started to think about some of the inanities that had popped out of her mouth in the few moments we'd been together after sex, and I found myself facing a harsh reality. When the flames of passion turned to embers, I might find that I was happier with the old relationship and its anonymous moments of ecstasy. I might look back fondly on our bodies, locked in the heat of passion, finally disentangling like the midair refuelers that are used to keep B-52's aloft. If I decided I didn't want a "committed relationship" after getting her to drop the boyfriend, I wasn't going to be able to go back to where we were. I would end up not getting fucked at all. I had to be careful before I did anything drastic.

೫

If you've ever tried to look up someone's number in the phone book when you don't know their first or last names, you'll have a good idea of what I was going through. But I had no other choice. Once I'd gone to Key West and started thinking about her as a real person with an identity, I was in trouble. I had lost a good part of the animal connection. I had become willful. I had made a decision. I didn't just want to see her whenever it happened, I wanted to have what I wanted when I wanted it. If I was going to see her on this basis then I had to know who she was. I had to call her up and make a date. And for that, all I could rely on was the White Pages. I held my county telephone book in my hand—all 593,428 names, not including the businesses, letting the pages run though my fingers. I sat with my legs tucked under my butt, the book in my lap, and my left hand cupped over my right. This is the classic Zen meditation position. I cleared my mind and nothing came. I would simply have to begin with *A* and see if anything rang a bell. I was at "Stella Agnew" when I saw I was in trouble. I'd be sitting there all day and all night and the next day and the next night. In the meanwhile, my eyes were growing heavy and I was falling asleep. I realized when I got to Stella Agnew's name that I'd have to reread the previous five columns, which went all the way back to "Arthur Adair." There was an "Arturo Adair," but that wasn't a girl's name, and a "Babs Adair," which certainly was. "Preston Adair" sounded familiar. Could that have been the name of her boyfriend? I tried to visualize her buzzer, but nothing was coming. Her boyfriend's name wasn't Preston Adair anymore than it was Alexsandr Solzhenitsyn.

I have an intuitive mind. I've been able to get out of some tough jams by instinctually sensing what my next move was going to be. I've been around the block a few times. What do I do when a muscle-bound gang of tattooed bikers approaches me and they're all swinging their nunchuks? What do I do when my car veers out of control and does a 360? For those of you who weren't born with the kind of intuition I was and who don't know what I'm talking about, the answer is, I get the hell out of there as fast as I can. But besides my intuitive side, I'm also mystically inclined. I have a tendency to believe that my mind is aligned with the higher forms of spiritual life that guide our universe—a trait known in the therapy trade as magical thinking. I'm the kind of guy who'll close his eyes and pick a name out of the hat. After all, I had already picked her out of the crowd once when I got back from Key West—unless of course the tomboyish-looking woman was just another hot fuck. But now I was letting my subjectivity get the better of me. Before I knew it, I would infer it was impossible to verify her existence at all, that she was an apparition, that she was a figment of my imagination, that she was all mind when the reality was SHE WAS ALL BODY! It's astounding the places the unfettered intellect will take one when it is not constrained by the guiding light of reason.

I threw the phone book on the ground and randomly opened it up. I was in the middle of the *T*'s: Richard Tnapsack, 141 Boyle; Susan Tnapsack, 616 Beech; Heather Tnapsack, 112 Smith. Smith and Heather had a familiar ring. I dialed. *This is Heather Tnapsack. I'm not home right now, but I'd really like to talk to you. Please leave your message after the beep.* The voice was enthusiastic, but overly firm. She sounded like an older woman who was afraid of not being heard. Just as I was about to put down my receiver, some one picked up on the other end.

"Hold on a minute. Lemme just turn off this machine. I can't never figure out where the switch is. Oh there. Hi."

The voice was definitely that of an older woman. The firmness had a shrill quality. It was her way of counterbalancing the tremors. But I didn't trust myself anymore. A person who was having a passionate affair with someone he wasn't sure even existed couldn't afford to leave any stone unturned. I was walking on thin ice, but I had to take a chance.

"I wanna shove my big hard rod up your soft hot honey pot."

"Oh baby, you're really turning me on. I'm sticking my finger in my pussy. Oooh, it's so hot. You wanna come over and eat me?"

"Will you let me shove my dick up your ass?"

"Oh yeah, turn me over on my stomach."

"Like a little doggy."

She barked. "Are you going to put a little leash around my neck and a muzzle around my mouth?"

"No, then you wouldn't be able to suck my cock."

I could tell I had dialed the wrong number. She was too old and hysterical sounding. My woman was more calm and collected when it came to talking dirty. This was like one of those experiments in chemistry where you add two chemicals together to see if a reaction will happen. If there had been a silence after I had started with the *I wanna shove my big hard rod* then I might have given Heather Tnapsack the benefit of the doubt. I'd known she wasn't the one, but I'd continued until her voice started to quiver, and I knew Heather Tnapsack was in all likelihood talking to me from a wheel chair or walker with a nurse's aide standing by her side. I realize there are no laws against liaisons with the elderly, but there is the law of nature. And when you're hard up enough to resort to talking about the doggy position with someone over 85, you're likely to get into trouble.

I politely told Heather Tnapsack I had the wrong number. I thanked her for her time. She was a little upset at first. She called me a "cracker asshole" and demanded we talk about it. She said she felt we were really getting along and wanted to know why I was pulling away. She even suggested we see the couples counselor she and her husband went to before he died. When I once again rejected her advances, she said, "You have a problem with intimacy," and slammed the phone down. She must have *69ed me because a minute later she called back screaming, "YOU CAN'T RUN AWAY FROM IT," and slammed the phone down again. I prayed she hadn't written my number down because once she received another incoming call, she'd lose the *69 capability on my number forever. She would then share my predicament—being raped and inseminated with a passion she was helpless to reciprocate. She couldn't find me, just as I couldn't find the fuck of my life. Was it Thoreau who said, "The mass of men lead lives of quiet desperation"?

It had long been my theory that earthquakes and volcanoes were subterranean manifestations of repressed sexuality. Moreover, most wars wouldn't have occurred if the natural expression of sexual desire hadn't been curtailed. Wars were then paraphilias or perversions, expressions of the desire for connection and security that had gone awry. Adversaries on the battlefield were lovers reaching out to each other, albeit in a somewhat angry and frustrated way. All of mankind—in fact all matter—inevitably seeks unification, and it is the disruption of this drive that causes all the misery in the universe. Isn't the Trojan War, a battle over a woman, the paradigm of such misplaced love? So I felt particularly guilty in exciting Heather Tnapsack and then pushing her away when I deduced how old she was. It may have been one drop in the bucket, but I was contributing to the strife that was gradually destroying not only the earth, but the universe.

However, worse than my remorse about Heather was my growing realization of the difficulty of the task at hand—locating my lover. If this were World War II and I were a member of the Gestapo, I could have ordered everyone in the city out of their houses on pain of being put before a firing squad. But even then I might not have recognized her. I only had one fact that didn't as yet qualify as a memory, since it was more concept than image. I was looking for a tomboyish woman, a woman who actually looked like a boy, whose hidden secret was that she fucked like a fiend. If for instance I had had the knowledge I would later have access to—that she was involved in the field of early childhood education as a part-time teacher in a Montessori school—my task would have been considerably easier. I would have had a hint, a clue, but unfortunately such information was not available to me at the time.

Vampires sucked blood; my lover had sucked not only my dick, but my soul. The life was seeping out of me. The more I looked at the columns of names in the phone book and the more I faced the reality of the Sisyphean task before me, the more I realized that without the pussy I craved, I no longer wanted to live. I was a dead man without her cunt. I felt a little like Jesus with his stigmata crying out, "My God why hast thou forsaken me?" After all, it was kind of up to her. She was the one who inevitably sought me out, and now, at a crisis point in our relationship, she was nowhere to be found. Furthermore, any remaining residues of our first purely animal attraction, which had pushed me in her direction, were deserting me, leaving me in a morass of mind that was little help in locating what was fast becoming a totally anonymous body. Admittedly it was only a crisis for me, as far as I knew. I didn't have any idea what her feelings were, anymore than I had an idea or memory of where she lived. I'd never said more than ten words to her at a time. On the other hand, I had to believe she was facing some of the same feelings I was. Her passion was equally powerful, and time had to be affecting her in some way. Unrequited passion, like unrequited love, only builds in intensity. That which has been lost always leaves more latitude for the imagination than the knowable. It's easy to idealize what you no longer possess. I was like a refugee who dreams of returning to the verdant fields he once plowed. I had to believe that since she was human she must have shared some of these same emotions.

Days passed. Bill could see how upset I was. Out of respect, he stopped glaring at the bulge in my pants. He produced one memorable meal after another. Romantic disappointments had previously resulted in a loss of appetite for me. It had happened with her during that meatloaf dinner when I first realized I was powerless to make our relationship more than it was—as it has happened all through my life when the girl I wanted didn't reciprocate my feelings. But now I became ravenously hungry. I gobbled up everything Bill cooked, cleaning off the last drops of gravy in our gravy boat with Bill's wonderful parsley-covered garlic bread. Then after dinner I'd sneak out and start all over again. One night I wandered downtown to the bus terminal where I'd first met Bill and landed in the local KFC, where I purchased the 24-piece family bucket of spicy. Another night, I indulged myself on ribs at Outback Steak House; on yet another, I gratified my desire for Big Macs by eating four in a row following the bass en croute dinner Bill had already served. My body was changing before my eyes. The simple thought of sex with her still produced a hard-on, but now a roll of fat was hanging on top of it. In fact, my hard-on looked like a beam on which my stomach rested for support. One night I took off my clothes and stared at myself in the full-length mirror in my closet. I'm fair of complexion—my skin was baby white as it had always been, but along with the creases of fat, I noticed that my body had become considerably more hirsute. The whiteness of my skin accentuated the tangled forest of graying hairs that covered my solar plexus. If she looked at me, if I became part of her life and she paid attention to the man she was fucking, if she got up in the morning and faced me sitting on the toilet with my roll of fat hanging over my thighs as I squeezed out the remains of my food bash the night before to an accompaniment of sputtering flatulence, would she continue to want me? Maybe I was better off not creating a real relationship in which my existence was so roundly acknowledged. I'd looked inside of myself and found a desire for a real relationship, but when I

took a good look at the outside of myself, I was full of doubt. I
didn't like what I saw.

It was 5:30 of a bitter-cold February morning. The phone
rang. As I rubbed my eyes, trying to get my bearings, I looked
out the window to see three dogs picking through garbage as
the wind rattled the pane. I knew it was her. And in spite of my
fatigue, I said to myself *remember, before she gets down on her knees
and starts sucking your cock, before she spreads her legs, playing with her
pussy and licking her own pussy juice off her fingers, remember, don't lose
control, remember what you've got to do. Look at her. Stop everything.
Your life is on the line. Don't let it be one more fuck fest which leaves
you exhausted, disoriented, and forgetful of what you've done or where
you've been.*

She had never called me before, and it was only in retrospect
that I wondered whether she just had better luck than I did
when it came to picking random names out of a telephone
book—or whether, as was probably the case, she had come by
the knowledge of my number through other means, like looking
at the driver's license in my wallet while I was in the bathroom
of her apartment. I had second thoughts. My mother had been
trapped in her body for years. Our sex was reassuring. It gave
me the illusion I had found a way of transcending my corporeal
essence. Yet now there was no choice. If she was going to locate
me, she was going to have to find out who and where I was.
And I was going to have to be someone and somewhere definite
(a condition I'd always equated with paralysis) in order to be
found.

"Tell me you wanna fuck me."

We hadn't talked dirty on the phone, but we'd sure done our
share of dirty talking. It was practically the only kind of talking
we did.

"I want you to fuck me like a savage."

Savage sounded curiously like *sandwich*. When I was a kid, I thought vaginas looked like sandwiches. You ate vaginas like you did sandwiches, but when you took this particular sandwich apart, it was just skin and hair with emissions and sweat, as opposed to mustard, ketchup, or mayonnaise. Bill turned leftover meatloaf into the most delicious sandwiches using fresh-baked challah bread, romaine lettuce, and radishes. What was all the excitement about? Okay, I was obviously immunizing myself against my fear of loss, but wasn't a cunt just another sandwich, and a fairly rotten one at that? A cunt is only prized by men because it's forbidden. The more difficult it is to gain entry, the more you want it. That's why you're not bothered by the air quality or noxious odor. It's no better than an asshole and, for that matter, how many times had each of us hungrily dived into each other's smelly anuses—blinded as we were by excitement? When you looked at the sex organ for what is was, you realized it was just skin, veins, and fatty tissue, maybe soft to the touch like a teddy bear, but no more special than say the fat hanging off the thigh or the arm. *Alas, poor Yorick!* A pussy, as it aged and lost its hair, was, in its makeup, no different from the hanging stubble-filled chin of an old woman. Why not dream of an old crone's hanging chin?

"We need to talk." I forced the words out like a judge handing down the death sentence of an innocent man.

"Yeah... fuck me in the ass and put yours right in my face and I'll lick it out."

"I feel I have a responsibility to you and to me to deal with our relationship."

"Sure we can, but I'm playing with my hot pussy." My dick was screaming. The tip was pushing up against my tight jockey underpants so hard it hurt. I thought my shaft was going to explode. I felt like I had varicose veins. I didn't pull my dick out of my pants, but I was afraid those veins were going to pop right out of the skin if she said one more word.

"Let me just suck on it for an hour or two. Then we'll talk. I'll lick the shaft and the sides of your balls. I've been exercising my tongue. I'll give you a hum job and a rimming you'll never forget."

"I don't even know your name, and yet all I think about is you. All relationships take work. We have something special...."

I don't remember what happened after this. I had tried, but the next thing I knew, I was back at her place sitting on her face with my cock between her tits. Her tongue was as firmly embedded in my asshole as my face was in her cunt. We both knew one thing: Ending the foreplay would bring about one of the hottest fucks we'd ever had. The anticipation was almost as delicious as fucking itself. But we wanted to extend it because we knew it would all be downhill after the fucking was over, unless we were both so knocked out by ecstasy that we wandered away in a fog, as we always had. We were, after all, adults, not teenagers who needed to sneak into closets or behind hedges to get forbidden thrills behind the back of the local authority figure.

After fucking her—and our fuck was every bit as hot as anything I could have imagined—I climbed off her sweaty body saying, "Now we need to deal with our relationship." It was a triumph of mind over matter. In the heat of our fucking, our bodies felt totally melded together. We were one. While the fuck continued, there was no me, no her. We were one self. Siamese twins who are physically joined suffer from the battle of their separate consciousnesses. Our physical union was brought about by a mental state that amongst other things, subdued the rising tide of self. There were no border police guarding the boundaries of personality. She was me, and I was her—even though we had yet to learn each others' names. Then it was over. We sat apart, still naked, staring. And for the first time I felt self-conscious. We were both looking over the goods.

"You're overweight."

"And you look more like a boy than a girl."

We threw our arms around each other.

"I'm Monica Cole."

"James Moran." Having been well brought up, I held my hand out to her after the introduction; she giggled as she shook it. I was too spent to say anything more than, "We should talk, soon."

Even though we had fucked our brains out, I felt as if it was going too far to ask for her number. I had her name—that was a start at least. Anyway, she looked like the kind of person who'd be listed. I certainly was. If I couldn't get her, she'd have no trouble getting me. I didn't know if she was going to want to continue seeing a guy whose roll of fat was supported by a perpetual hard-on, and I had to decide if I wanted to spend my life with Peter Pan. However juicy her pussy, Monica Cole was a woman who didn't have a curve in her body. She could have been the poster girl for a ruler company. I'd gained a lot of weight, but she was wafer thin with a chest that was decidedly lacking in drama. Nevertheless, before I could answer Bill when I rushed through the front door and he said, "Guess what we're having… meatloaf," I was on the phone calling information.

"I'd like the telephone number of a Monica Cole. It's a residence." There was the longest wait. *Please be patient while we look for your number.* The automated voice kept repeating the same message. While I was waiting for Monica's number, another call was trying to come through. What if I was on the phone talking with someone I couldn't get rid of when I finally got an operator? I pushed the "flash" button on my phone.

"Jim?" It was her. Bill was pointing towards the door. I could see him mouthing the words "I have to shop," but I didn't dare interrupt the conversation and he left in a huff.

"Actually it's James, nobody calls me Jim." I knew I'd said the wrong thing the minute the words came out of my mouth. We were no longer simply a cock and cunt. We were people. Human personality is like religion. It can be a source of great wisdom and solace, but it also creates divisions, conflicts, and sometimes even wars. Personalities, like religions, had often done more harm than good, and now that more than sex was involved, now that our personalities had entered into the relationship, we were already experiencing conflict. It was oh so much easier when few words were exchanged and all we did was fuck.

"I wanted to invite you out to dinner."

"Isn't that usually the prerogative of the male?"

"I thought you wanted to discuss our relationship. Do you want me to hang up? You can call me back." I don't like being challenged and I didn't like the tone of her voice, which was decidedly snide. Recently, I'd watched a documentary on the Discovery Channel about the mating pattern of porcupines. Apparently the male urinates on the woman. If she likes it, they fuck. In this case it felt like the reverse, and to extend the analogy, I wasn't enjoying her needles. I was paying for my shyness as I had ever since I was a kid. I should have asked for her number right away. Then I would have been on the horn, and we wouldn't have been experiencing the kind of role reversal that was creating confusion from the get-go. It's hard moving from a purely physical relationship to one in which you deal with the love partner as a real individual who could end up being the beneficiary to your life insurance policy. Monica Cole was a phantom whom I was trying to integrate into my life, but the mind/body problem was already turning into a sticky issue. Once she took my dick out of her mouth and started to talk, the hot cunt turned into a raving bitch.

I simply hung up the phone. I'd let her cool her tootsies. Then I'd call back and start all over again—but when I *69ed her, I got a busy signal. The bitch had taken the phone off the hook. I was so irritated with her I forgot to write down the number. All of a sudden there was a ring. I didn't pick right up. I wanted to sound firm yet loving, and certainly not vindictive. I would be understanding, even therapeutic.

"Hey, it's Pete. May I please speak to Bobby." It was an adolescent's voice.

"Sorry, kid, you got the wrong number."

All of a sudden I realized, my ass was grass. If I *69ed, I was going to get Pete. I grabbed the phone.

Verizon nationwide 411 listing, the computerized voice said.

"I'd like the telephone number of a Monica Cole." The wait seemed to be endless.

Please wait while an operator looks for that number... thank you for waiting. Your request is still being processed. Thank you for continuing to hold. Please wait while an operator looks for that number. The same message repeated itself over and over again, until after one final *thank you for continuing to hold,* the voice of a human finally came on the line.

"Was that Monica Cole? How do you spell that name?"

"Monica like it sounds, *M-o-n-i-c-a,* and Cole like coal mine."

"Checking under Monica Coal. I don't see any listing. Is it a business or a residence?"

I felt like saying business. Why don't you check under hot pussy? After all, Verizon had made me wait; I should be able to say what I wanted.

"How are you spelling that Cole?"

"Like coal mine."

"Have you ever heard of anyone whose name is spelled c-*o-a-l*?"

"Sir, you said 'coal like coal mine.'"

"You shouldn't take everything so literally. People don't always say what they mean. It's *C-o-l-e,* I'm sure, like Nat King Cole, Natalie Cole, and most other people who call themselves Cole. If you come across a *C-o-a-l* in all your years as an information operator, and I'm sure you'll have a long and distinguished career, I would appreciate it if you would call me." I was beginning to lose my patience. I wasn't even sure I wanted Monica Cole's number. I was in love with a hot pussy, but I wasn't convinced I wanted to spend my life with Monica Cole.

"Checking under Monica *C-o-l-e*, I'm not showing a number listed under that name."

I slammed the phone down in frustration. They tell you when it's an unlisted number. If it had been unlisted I would have had something to work with, but I was back to ground zero.

It was then that the phone rang again.

"I really don't appreciate your behavior."

"Oh, I'm so happy you called back." I adopted the sweetest, most understanding voice in my repertoire, the voice of a man who didn't want anything to get in the way of his fucking. "I tried to call you back, but you weren't listed."

"Why didn't you *69 me?"

"I wanted to *69 you very badly, but Pete called looking for Bobby."

"I should have told you… I'm of Swedish extraction. My parents were immigrants. It was Coole. You don't pronounce the final *e* and it sounds like "cool." In high school they used to tease me and call me Monica Cooley. You know, like those guys who drive the rickshaws. I had enough problems being a gangly kid whose parents had strange accents, so I took away an *o* to change the pronunciation to Cole so the kids wouldn't make fun of me."

This still didn't explain why she wasn't listed. I felt like saying *they wouldn't dare make fun of you if they knew what a great fuck you were*, but it was neither the time nor—since we were separate—the place.

"Who's Pete anyway?"

"A wrong number, but what part of Sweden were your parents

from? I'm a great Bergman fan. When I first saw movies like *Through a Glass Darkly* (1961) and *The Silence* (1963) I developed this infatuation for anything Swedish. These are depressing films about the death of God, but I just fell in love with the lifestyle. I don't speak the language, but I used to pretend I was Swedish. I'd carry on imaginary conversations with Liv Ullman in the mirror and pretend I was Sven Nyqvist, Bergman's cinematographer. I developed a lilt in my voice and finished words on a higher note than they started, thinking that would make me sound Swedish. I associated the accent with wisdom, and I affected this world-weary air, which I took to be part and parcel of the weight Swedish people carried on their shoulders—a weight that I thought derived from a higher level of consciousness. I longed to have rings under my eyes like Max von Sydow. When I was in grad school I went to a Swedish tailor who made suits and jackets that would have been considered fashionable in Stockholm, but the women at the University of Miami didn't get it. It was a party school back then. You wanted to at least look like you were on the football team. I walked around like I was in a state of existential crisis. Hardly anyone even got that I was trying to seem Swedish. One of my roommates once accused me of being an exchange student who was trying to act like an American, though he had no idea where I was an exchange student from. Most people just thought I was weird. But here I am going on and on."

"My father constantly attacked my mother. He hit her when he got drunk. I used to try to get between them to break up the fights. He was obsessed with clothes and appearances. He hated the way she dressed. He accused her of intentionally making herself look like an old maid."

"I wished you hadn't said that. I may be guilty of over idealization, but I still have a residual affection for things Swedish. Look at their excellent health care system. It's hard for me to believe that a Swedish male would behave like such a Neanderthal."

"Look at how they hounded poor Bergman about his taxes. This is how the Swedish treat the greatest film and stage director of the twentieth century! I would examine your affection for such a culture."

"Well obviously your disaffection is the result of your own childhood traumas."

"You're pathologizing me and I resent it." It was the first time she'd actually raised her voice.

I was not only missing our old interactions, I had sunk into despair. The feeling was biblical. I was reminded of Lot's wife, who turned into a pillar of salt. There was no going back. How would the contentious pseudo-intellectual be restored to being the great fuck who abandoned herself to my prick, screaming for me to plunge it into her ass after it had already been in her cunt and mouth? You can't turn a pickle back into a cucumber.

"I'm sorry. Let me make it up to you by shoving my hard cock down your throat." It was a leap of faith. I totally didn't feel like it, but I was desperate. I needed to jump-start the old relationship.

"I really don't appreciate your attempt to sexualize me when we are having a difference."

My prick shriveled up so far inside of me that I thought it would become part of my intestines.

"All men care about is power. That's why we live in such a strife-ridden world. You take sex, which is a nice thing, and use it as a means of violence against women."

"Oy yoy yoy." I was feeling faint, and then I could feel a hot surge in my stomach and the galloping that foretells gastrointestinal crisis. I ran to the bathroom and began shitting my guts out. If I didn't kill myself, I would be ten pounds lighter when the whole thing ended, if it ever did. The phone was still off the hook. I could hear Monica's voice screaming through the sound of the cascading diarrhea. If you've ever seen those movies where a family is trapped in a maelstrom when lightning strikes, the wind howls and the heavens open up, wreaking their vengeance on man and reminding him of his lowly place in the great chain of being, you will understand the level of turbulence that filled the apartment. Fumes from my stomach suffused the atmosphere. Anyone who walked into my apartment would have been sickened. Then all at once, as in those classic old movies, the storm passed. I stopped. I felt cleansed and refreshed. I felt as if I'd gotten my old self back. Not only had the toxic substances been eliminated from my stomach, I had been purged of the violent emotions brought on by the conversation. I was relaxed. I felt in control. I was ready to deal with the problems in our relationship.

Now that I had stopped the groaning that had accompanied my ordeal, I could plainly hear Monica screaming into the receiver, "What's wrong, James? James, please pick up. Jim, come to the phone. James or Jim—which do you prefer?"

Calmly, I picked up the receiver.

"It's hard to talk over the phone. Would you like to get together for dinner?"

"I'd like you to fuck me in my ass and mouth." The old Monica had returned, but as much as my cock was screaming for satisfaction, I knew that I had to take advantage of the widening of the fault, to extend the natural disaster analogy. Our tumultuous conversation had opened something up. Getting back to our old relationship was simpler, safer, more immediately satisfying. She was scared, and so was I, but it was too easy.

"I really feel we need to talk."

"I wanna fuck." I could tell we were headed for another battle of the wills.

"I tell you what. Let's talk, and then I promise I'll give you a really hard fuck. I'll tit fuck you, I'll fuck you in your ass and cunt, and I'll come all over your face." Plainly she took my willingness to talk dirty as a sign of compromise because she meekly said, "Okay."

"It's just very difficult to talk over the phone," I repeated. I told her I would look in my *Zagat's* and get back to her. I wanted to find some place nice for our first dinner together.

"What do you like?"

"Game," she replied, "but I have to go. My boyfriend just walked in." I could tell something had changed. I had gotten what I wanted. Now I was talking to a real person over the phone. If the instinctual pre-verbal side to our relationship had been waning, now it was just about gone. There might be exceptions, but in general, you forswear the animal connection that finds you mindlessly in bed with someone once you cross the magic line where you use the phone to make dates.

We met in a place called The Golden Cock. The Golden Cock turned out to be a gay all-you-can-eat barbecue place that became a disco after midnight. Some of these gay places don't like to encourage heterosexual couples, but The Golden Cock was extreme, displaying roughly the level of tolerance for heterosexuals that the whites did for blacks in Alabama when George Wallace was governor. It was understood that the bathrooms were for gays only; the line of guys waiting to get fucked in the ass wasn't too happy when Monica and I joined them. Monica had insisted on getting her mouth on my dick after we both finished our appetizers, and considering that her repartee was a mixture of feminist admonishments and phone-sex-advertising-level eroticism, I was happy to oblige. For all her sexual abandon, Monica turned out to be a control freak. If she was going to leave the security of her current relationship, she needed something in writing, whether it be a marriage certificate or a prenuptial agreement.

"I'm not going to fuck my brains out for ten years and end up with a dried-up pussy and nothing to show for it." How could someone fuck so beautifully yet utter such streams of ugly invective? Sometimes people show the worst side of themselves so that the good side is like the raspberry filling in a stale jelly donut. What had made Monica so cynical and distrusting of life? She'd been born with a pussy that was one of the seven wonders of the world. People sell their souls to get sexual equipment like that. When it came to sex she displayed the startling ability to be the caboose and the engine all at the same time. She could take it as well as she could give it, an admirable talent for a person of either sex.

But like a lot of talented people, she had her destructive side. She obviously couldn't handle her gifts and lessened the effect of her sexual brilliance with some of the stupidest invective that had ever filled a man's ears. I wasn't ready to sign my furnishings over to her. Yet I wasn't willing to give up hope that the saliva-filled mouth meeting my cock was also a sign of a warmth and tenderness she was too defensive to show in our verbal encounters. Underneath she might be as vulnerable and forthcoming emotionally as she was sexually. I'm well hung enough, but now what was required was that I hang in; I was looking for a pay-off that could be as explosive emotionally as any of the scenes in Noel Coward's filmic masterpiece of romantic longing, *Brief Encounter* (1948)—minus, of course, the film's glamorization of unconsummated love. All I wanted out of Monica was the intensity of an unrealizable romantic passion that was at the same time realizable in an everyday relationship that offered financial and emotional security as well as health benefits. In the meantime I settled for a memorable fuck in the farthest stall of The Golden Cock. Not even the long line of gays waiting impatiently to suck each others cocks seemed to mind, especially when Monica explained, "It's okay, he's only fucking me in the ass."

Soon after pulling out and leaving the bathroom, I asked for a check. We agreed it had been a lovely night, but both of us also agreed that it was important not to act impulsively in terms of deciding what kind of relationship we'd have.

"I love to fuck you, but I don't like you," she said. "Just kidding."

I didn't like her at all, but as long as my dick was shoved into her ass, pussy, or mouth, I was in a state that can only be described as rapturous.

The weather had already begun to change, and by the time I got home from dinner, spring had arrived. When I awakened the next morning, I breathed in the sweet fragrance that betokens the first flowering of the season. The bare branches of the old oak outside my apartment were now covered with buds, and without going on with a stereotypic cataloguing of seasonal changes, suffice it to say the once frozen streets—previously devoid of life—now bore witness to chirping as the first migrations of birds descended from the skies. My life lay before me. The first hint of mild weather filled the streets with young women in abbreviated attire. Thick woolen sweaters and turtlenecks were replaced by revealing halter tops. Newly pierced belly buttons were paraded and rear views, with their prominently displayed thong waist bands, provided a tantalizing peek into the freedom of our current youth culture. I was no longer young, but I wondered if perhaps I had limited my horizons. Monica had stirred something up in me, but to believe she was the only woman who could provide me with a life of sexual satisfaction was actually placing too great a burden on her. Did I need to experiment more before I put all my eggs in one basket? I didn't want to experiment more. But if I was going to settle down with Monica, I had to accept her, warts and all (unlike the character in

Hawthorne's short story, "The Birthmark," who ends up killing the woman he loves when he tries to remove the one thing that mars her perfection). My need to edit every word that came out of her mouth was no fairer to her than it was to me.

◌ঙ

We were taking a break. I wanted to see her, but I didn't. Within the context of the relationship, time increasingly came to feel relative. Days could go by without my realizing it, and yet I had afternoons when I wished Monica would call, and the hours passed agonizingly slowly. I would pick up the phone then put it down fearing her boyfriend was home. One day I got a call from Monica at one of those extraordinary moments when I wasn't even thinking of her pussy. I was caught totally off guard, and for a moment I didn't even know who she was. If truth be told, it wasn't the word *Monica* that flitted through my consciousness when I thought of her, it was the feeling of being engulfed by a hot, hairy thing that surrounded my hard dick, with muscles like hydraulic clamps that sucked me in almost against my will, and at times, apparently against my better judgment. I may even have asked, "Monica who?" before I blurted out, "Just kidding." If I was kidding, she didn't find it funny. Her voice was tentative when she asked if I was doing anything that night and if I wanted to go back to The Golden Cock.

"I don't know. I wasn't that crazy about the food." It was going to be one of those conversations where you're damned if you do and damned if you don't. Telling her my truthful opinion about The Golden Cock only showed my ambivalence about the relationship—but if I didn't tell her, I would be setting a precedent. I'd be hiding my feelings. What was the point of our cementing a bond based on lies?

I wanted to fuck her, but I didn't want to get together with her—which is a pragmatic way of explaining our existential dilemma. The form the conflict was taking was an inability to decide where to eat.

"I'm not that hungry right now," I said. There was an angry silence at the other end of the line, followed by a hang up.

I immediately called her back.

"I will be hungry," I said. "So let me check my *Zagat's*. I don't mind The Golden Cock."

"Look, tonight may not be a good idea anyway. I'm having my period."

We weren't great conversationalists, it turned out, but we had other things. Some people are capable of great exchanges of words, others are better with fluids. We fell in the latter category. It was the cross we had to bear.

I decided to give in, and we agreed to meet at The Golden Cock. Even as a boy, having a passionate first affair with my mother, I learned that when it came to women you had to make them feel they were getting their way. It assured them you cared. Going back to The Golden Cock was like a reunion; everyone remembered us. I felt like an honorary member of the club— the club of gay men that is. Our spirits were high and we felt accepted. Wafted away on the cloud of good feeling, and despite her period, Monica insisted on retiring to our favorite stall in the men's room—which now felt like a second home—before we'd even ordered. Just for the record, The Golden Cock has wonderful goose. The portions aren't big, but they're thick and crispy. My last memory before our candlelit dinner was served was of Monica impaled on my cock. (I remember thinking that she had been lying about her period.)

She reminded me of the time my mother took me to the rodeo after she had blown me at the Hyatt in Cincinnati. I was very much in love with her back then, and when I saw that cowboy riding his bucking bronco I felt an immediate compulsion to have my mother on top, riding me the same way. It was a fantasy that became a reality when we returned to our room after the rodeo. Now in the bathroom with a constant stream of gay couples fucking each other up the ass and getting or giving blowjobs or golden showers and Monica crying out, "More, more, more, harder, harder, harder," I was reminded of the halcyon days of my youth, when it was just mom and me against the world. The only difference was that life was simpler back then. There was none of the *sturm and drang* that Monica and I had stirred up. You don't choose whether you're going to have a long term relationship with your mother. She's your mother! You don't have to worry about things like commitment. Grilled cheese was my favorite sandwich when I was a kid, and mom made great grilled cheese sandwiches. She'd always have a buttery one waiting for me with a cold glass of milk when I got home from school. After I was done eating and watching television, she'd walk into the kitchen naked or with some new lingerie she wanted to try on for me, and I'd go down on her as she stood by the table pretending to look over my homework.

When Monica and I walked out of our stall, there was clapping from the line of gay men who were waiting to relieve themselves on each other. I don't know too many heterosexual couples whom gay people, with their high testosterone levels, would consider in the same league when it comes to intensity of sex. I had come out of my usual post-coital Monica haze, not knowing who or where I was, to experience feeling flattered and successful about something that I couldn't presently ascertain. Here were all these strangers with their cock rings, their tattoos, their pierced urethras, noses, lips, eyebrows, and even toes, all clapping wildly for us. The reception wasn't quite as enthusiastic in the dining room.

The Golden Cock had a double standard. On the surface they were a four-star restaurant with slightly fey-looking waiters and a maitre d' who wore a fez. The bathroom was like the satanic force of the Manichean heresy; for both the staff and patrons, that was obviously the appeal. They liked to feel they were sneaking away to do something naughty. The dining room was quite formal looking for a barbecue joint, with its China services and thick white candles on the tables (one of the men on line in the bathroom had already swiped one of these, and as we passed him he was in the process of covering it with that manna of the gods, Astroglide, before shoving it up his own ass like an oversized suppository while waiting for an empty stall). In my disoriented state I had re-entered this dining room with my dick hanging out of my pants. I wouldn't even have noticed if the maitre d', proudly displaying his "I love Michel Foucault" button, hadn't scampered over to tell me, "Appropriate attire is required in this area." Luckily this was a sophisticated crowd. Heads turned as we walked by the two tables closest to the men's room, but before the maitre d' even got to me, the dining room had become impervious to my indiscretion and was awash again in the high-pitched gay chatter that sounds like a coop full of free-range chickens.

Despite the warnings of the management and my protestations that we needed to talk, Monica couldn't keep her hands off of me. No sooner had I stuck my dick back into my opened fly and sat down than Monica was grabbing for it. At one point, just before her appetizer came (a suggestive and beautifully displayed selection of pepperonis and salamis from around the world), she actually got annoyed because my cock was caught in the piss hole of my jockey briefs. She tugged so hard that I let out a cry, stopping all the polite conversation that had surged around us since the first interruption caused by our dramatic entry. Monica was so frustrated she started to suck on one of the sausages until, giving up all pretenses, she simply excused herself saying, "I lost my earring," stuck her head under the table, and put the real thing in her mouth. My cum dripped out of her lips as she came up from the floor, but she insisted on a passionate kiss nevertheless. I had ordered the peppercorn pâté, which was garnished with gherkins. One of the rare pleasures in life is smelling your own body fluids on someone else's lips, and the condiments provided with my pâté were no competition for the aroma emanating from Monica's mouth. I should add that in spite of her tomboyish appearance, which made her fit right in with the occasional dykes who were part of an exchange program that The Golden Cock ran with its sister restaurant, Lady Fingers, Monica had wonderfully voluptuous lips from which my seed hung with romantic, almost mythic abandon. Sitting in The Golden Cock with little droplets of cum on her lips, cheek, and forehead, she looked like Aphrodite after a nervous breakdown.

Monica was looking at me with love in her eyes—the lashes of which were also caked together with ejaculate. And if it hadn't been for the extraordinary events that had gone on in the bathroom of The Golden Cock and later under the table, the pungent odors they produced, and the singular effect they had on both of our appearances, we would have looked like your typically smitten couple.

Obstacles have presented themselves to lovers from the beginning of time. The difficulty can result in tragedy or joy. Romeo and Juliet were separated by the enmity between their warring families, but I had never read of a pair of lovers separated by the kind of transcendent and ecstatic sex that obliterated their identities, leaving them in a state of temporary amnesia after each consummated act. Most lovers overcome obstacles to achieve consummation. We had consummated our love. That wasn't the problem; the obstacles came after. But now we had arrived at a turning point. After much difficulty in even getting each other's telephone numbers, we were starting to form a bond. As I stared across the table at Monica, I realized how much I loved her, and I was wondering if she was feeling the same way about me until she opened her mouth and blurted out, "I want you to urinate on me." I explained that I had never been turned on by golden showers—despite the fact that I'd once offered to urinate on her (later I would understand her change in attitude from the initial distaste she expressed at the mention of golden showers as resulting from her years of experience being peed on by pre-schoolers). I'd seen guys lying in urinals in the bathroom of The Golden Cock, looking as if they were taking the sacraments as streams of urine splattered over their faces, and I was nonplussed. I can understand wanting to get fucked in the ass; being someone who enjoys Greeking, I have empathy for the recipient of the pleasure. But I'd never wanted to piss on someone, and I couldn't understand why anyone would want to be bathed in foul-smelling uric acid.

"Golden showers are the blowjobs of tomorrow." Monica's Jesuitical side always came out in these discussions. As far as I can tell, her attitude about sex was Hegelian. She believed in a dialectic, a chain of historical necessity that defined human behavior. But this intellectual side to her made me uncomfortable in the end. Everything was an argument. She fucked with the greatest abandon, but when she tried to talk about our relationship she sounded like a whining academician writing a feminist revisionist polemic that managed to be masochistic in content and sadistic in tone. In short, she lacked heart.

Ever one to take an argument to its logical conclusion, I prosecuted the meaning of the metaphor.

"You're saying people are going to relinquish fellatio?"

"No, no more than they've relinquished the missionary position. In our current day and age you suck someone off and it's all over. The person who's been sucked either falls asleep watching television or looks for excitement elsewhere. Ditto intercourse. Most men are not going to be able to have a second orgasm within the next ten or fifteen minutes. It's alienating and disappointing for women who want to keep making love. The golden shower is a way of prolonging the sexual experience. Some novelist is going to come around and do for golden showers what *Portnoy's Complaint* did for blowjobs."

She looked up at me with an expression that said *what do you think?*

"That's very interesting."

"I'd love nothing better than to fill my mouth with your hot sis. C'mon, this place is too uptight. Let's go in the men's room. I'll let you piss all over my face and tits. You can even take a leak on top of my head."

Now I suddenly felt at home. When she was being overly abstract, Monica's words were sterile. She was detached. She was no longer the person I thought I was beginning to know, but now what was coming out of her mouth was the real Monica, the woman who writhed both under and on top of me, whose cunt could make any room smell like a Chinatown fish market.

The minute we walked into the men's room she threw all modesty to the wind. Jacking up her skirt, pulling down her thong, she lay on her back in the first urinal. The Golden Cock's nightly slave auction must have started since the bathroom was empty. I'd plainly been holding it in because the first golden shower I ever gave kept going on and on and on. Monica might have been sitting under a waterfall; my stream literally bounced off her face. I peed so long that I accidentally flushed—out of obedience to my inner clock—when my bladder was only halfway emptied. I apologized, but Monica didn't seem to mind. When I hesitated, holding my stream in for a moment after pulling the flusher, she cried out, "More, more, you fucking bastard. I wanna be really humiliated." I didn't take it personally. She always employed the kind of language used to describe torture techniques of the Inquisition when she was out of control with excitement. I wasn't surprised to hear her screaming that she wanted to be humiliated any more than I would have if she demanded that she be flagellated.

After I was done, I walked over to the next urinal. There are always a few drops left at the end, and I shook them off as I always do after taking a whiz. It's something my mother taught me as a little boy that has come in handy in social situations. I'm not one of these guys who walks around with a spot in his crotch when he is wearing light-colored trousers. This display of my caringness for the feelings of others has not gone unappreciated. When friends look at my crotch or the tips of my shoes—other places where men typically splatter—they often thank me for my courtesy.

When I was done, I held my hand out to Monica and lifted her out of the urinal. I was so turned on by the pissing, I stopped her when she started to pull her panties up. I turned her around so she was facing the urinal, pushed her forward so that she had to brace herself against the wall in order to avoid falling in, and shoved my finger right up her ass. She let out a scream that would have awakened the dead, and as a busboy and waiter ran in to see what was wrong, I thrust my rocket-hard dick straight up her ass.

"Kill me with your dick." In spite of the piss all over Monica's face, we couldn't keep our hands off each other. We started to make out wildly until Monica said, "Okay, it's your turn, big guy."

I lay down on the floor of the bathroom right there and then. She squatted over me and took what could only be called a passionate piss, in which she used her stream to make figure eights all over my face and chest. Heaven is the only word to describe the experience. If she never said a word to me again, that moment—when I was staring up into her parted labia and asshole, and a strong yellow stream was coming at me with the vibrancy of the life force itself—would have epitomized everything that made our love as singular and powerful as it was. I've always said that love is like a river, and in that moment—on the dirty tiled floor of The Golden Cock, with the swish of urine emanating from her and its steady stream flowing with the pressure of a spigot in a luxury apartment building—I knew what they meant when they said *you're in for the long haul*. If this was what commitment entailed, if this was what it took to be in a relationship, then I wanted it. We'd had some rough times and some misunderstandings, especially when it came to verbal communication. I had mistakenly thought that the lack of rapport we had when it came to words, ideas, and feelings was an indication that we weren't right for each other. There was a lesson to be learned in this, not only for myself, but for others: Never judge a book by its cover. What is said rarely has anything to do with reality. Words are a mask. I only have to think back to my first experiences of sex in high school. I'd be on top of a girl and I'd ask, "Do you want to fuck?" She'd naturally say no or, "No, don't do that," when I first tried to remove her skirt or blouse, but two minutes later her panties and bra would be off and her mouth would be dancing up and down my shaft in that frantic way that women have when they both want to be fucked and want to hold off and tease to increase the intensity of the final moment when the prick, reddened with excitement, is shoved up their wet, hot cunt holes.

Both of us knew at that moment on the bathroom floor of The Golden Cock that there was no turning back. We were in it for keeps, but if we were indeed in it for the long haul, I was going to have to give up Bill, and she was going to have to move out of her pad or have her boyfriend move out. We were going to have to climb out of the puddle of cum, piss, and cunt juice that was the paradise we created whenever we got together, to deal with the realities of our lives. For instance, Monica had the lease on the apartment, but while the sofa and the dining room table were hers, the bed belonged to her boyfriend, and the kitchenware, it turned out, was also his. Monica felt she couldn't deal with the vicissitudes of our existence together until she shopped. After we had purchased any beds, chairs, or dishes she needed, she would feel more secure in telling her boyfriend she was leaving him. In fact, she argued, having furniture delivered to her house would be an excellent way of informing her boyfriend she was leaving him. The idea made little sense as far as I was concerned (from my point of view it would have been more practical to tell our respective companions and then do the shopping), but I had come to accept the fact that the woman I loved could be a deeply muddled thinker when she wasn't talking about blowjobs or golden showers. Like a blind person, she had compensated for her deficiencies in one area with great sensitivity and awareness in others—one of which was sex.

The waterbed was an expense that we both immediately agreed on. It epitomized Mies van der Rohe's Bauhaus form-follows-function idea in that the choice of décor was dictated by the activity that took up the greatest amount of our time together. Another couple might have lavished attention on a library, television room, or kitchen, but we never discussed books, watched TV, or cooked. We knew our life together would be about take-out Chinese food and hours of fucking. I could just see the piles of cartons with brown sauce stains dripping down the sides, lining the shelves of our refrigerator like tombstones in a cemetery.

The waterbed would also be an unequivocal statement. The minute that bed arrived, her boyfriend had to know Monica was making a choice between the sexless one-fuck-a-week life they had lived and the deeper sexuality that was so dominant a part of her nature. Monica had been living a lie. She had tried to appear like a modest, upstanding citizen instead of an unspayed bitch in heat. She'd been leading a double life. When she'd fucked her brains out with me, she'd been cheating on her boyfriend. When she was trying to be something she was not, she was cheating on herself.

I arrived with my bags soon after the boyfriend had left. Monica's eyes were red from crying, but the minute she saw me she unzipped my fly and started to suck on my cock. She had me lie down on the bed, and she held it in her mouth, sucking on it not as if she were giving me a blowjob, but with the short little suction movements of the lips that infants employ when they are sucking on a pacifier. My dick was plainly a great solace to her in her moment of grief.

My parting from Bill turned out to be more wrenching than I'd expected. I knew he had grown very attached to me, and I came close to letting him suck my cock just one time as a goodbye gift, but I asked myself *what's once? If he does it once, he's going to want to do it again and again, and he's likely to become a pain in the ass both figuratively and literally.* Still, having a person willing to lavish so much unswerving attention on you is a real gift. I had been fortunate in finding the unconditional love from Bill I'd never even gotten from my mother, who treated me more as a lover than a son (when I was good in bed she liked me, when I wasn't so good she was cool and removed). The kind of care and love I got from Bill reminded me very much of Maxey, my old poodle. And when I told Bill I was moving in with Monica, I felt very much the way I did when I put Maxey to sleep. I couldn't even look at Bill. I walked out, sobbing loudly once I got down the stairs onto the street so he wouldn't hear me. Bill and I had been through so much together. I knew Monica couldn't continue to see her boyfriend; that would have been too complicated. But Bill and I had never become lovers, and it occurred to me that once things settled down he could still cook for us or even be our maid.

附

Bill and I went through a tough period when I first moved in with Monica. He called all the time and threatened to commit suicide, but once he was reassured that he would play a major role in our lives, he calmed down. I let Bill live in my old apartment, which I was going to keep until I was absolutely sure Monica and I could successfully live together. That would be his remuneration; in the event I gave the apartment up, I'd pay Bill a salary large enough for him to get his own place. Soon after Bill had adjusted to his new circumstances, he'd started to buy exercise tapes; I also offered to pay for him to take courses in aerobics at our local junior college so that he could live out another one of his dreams: To become an exercise guru like Richard Simmons. I'd encouraged Monica to sign up for a seminar in communication arts at the same place. I thought they might even commute together.

My only real problem was a career that put me on the road for half the year. For starters, I would be doing *Bye Bye Birdie* in Cincinnati during June and we'd have to figure something out. We'd tried phone sex on several occasions, but it reminded me of Plato's cave. We didn't have a verbal relationship to begin with, and sex that depended on the romantic language of seduction bore a pale relation to the real thing. Monica and I were as capable of cursing and getting down and dirty as anyone. That kind of verbal banter was no problem; it was a strong point in our relationship, in fact. But statements like, *Fuck me up the ass, Shove your finger up my hole, I wanna fuck your stinking pussy, I'm gonna come on your face*, were more effective for us as loving additions to a physical act. I had learned from experience. Saying, *I'm going to plug up your shit hole* into a receiver hardly has the emotional power of actually shoving a part of myself up into someone's tight ass.

I can't say that Monica and I had ever gotten to know each other like normal couples who use language to get close. When I got back from *Bye Bye Birdie*, we started to fuck in the same demented way we always had. I didn't know whether I was returning from my trip or leaving, and I had no idea at one point how I got where I was in life—specifically, the sunken center of our new waterbed. If the first few months we were living together was a litmus test, then familiarity had not only not brought about contempt or the usual lethargy and loss of appetite that couples complain about when the chase is over, it had brought an even higher level of intensity to our relationship. While many of our early encounters had found me wandering barefoot in the streets with my pockets hanging out of my pants, this new sexuality produced a state somewhere between delirium and levitation. We began to see ourselves as privileged. Few people ever have the opportunity to use their bodies as we were lucky enough to do. If it occurs, it's a once-in-a-lifetime event, and yet here we were having it every day. So it was lucky we had decided to finally move in together. No longer did I need to worry about what had happened to me every time I fucked her and my brains out. Nor did I need to spend my time trying to reconstitute the face behind the pussy bringing me such joy.

Our first real problem was the waterbed. On several occasions we actually fucked so hard it exploded. The mess leaked through the floor onto the downstairs neighbors—a young couple who fucked a lot because they were trying to get pregnant. Sometimes, as I put my dick into Monica's snatch, I heard other cries along with her usual moaning and thought to myself *this place really is beginning to sound like the primate room at the zoo.*

After several complaints and a threatening lawyer's letter, we both realized we needed to see someone, and I found a counselor who specialized in the problems of couples whose sex lives are too good. Usually people seek marital counseling when they have issues like unfaithfulness, lack of desire, impotence, or frigidity. We needed to seek help because our sexual attraction to each other was so powerful that it might harm the environment. We were like a tornado or a hurricane: When we were fucking we didn't know what we were doing and we tended to eradicate anything or anyone that crossed our path. The counselor's name was Martin Shapiro. He'd been a career military man who had honed his skills in couples counseling while serving in Vietnam. He'd been the highest-ranking Jewish marriage counselor in the history of the United States Army. He'd attained the level of Brigadier General. And even though he was an MD psychoanalyst by training, he was still addressed as General Shapiro.

Talk about warring couples, the first session we had with him, he told us the story of the Special Forces captain who was married to a high-level member of the Viet Cong. As unbelievable as it may sound, Shapiro claimed he was able to create a trusting relationship between a couple who, though they would literally be firing on each other during the day, desired the kind of domestic arrangement where they could cook for each other and make passionate love after returning home in the evening. That wasn't our problem. We weren't adversarial (except when we talked)—we were explosive. Our sexuality, General Shapiro claimed, had something in common with the fusion reaction that created the hydrogen bomb.

I tried to describe the unique conditions under which Monica and I had first met in order to give General Shapiro a real feeling for the roots of our relationship and what it was like, but before I even got another word out, he cut me off. My understanding is that therapists usually like patients to come forth, but I immediately got the feeling that however truthful General Shapiro's observations were, he was more interested in being the one to do the talking and more interested in relating our experiences to his own. Shapiro seemed to subscribe to the notion that patients were like children who should be seen, but not heard.

"A hydrogen bomb is detonated by a smaller nuclear device like an atom bomb. Once the chain reaction starts, there's no stopping it. That's what I see here. Independently, the two of you are harmless bits of organic matter, but putting you two together, you become lethal. Waterbeds break, neighbors are frightened, you find yourselves wandering in the streets not knowing who you are. The question is what sets you off, what's your atom bomb? Once we can defuse that, then we can explore what goes on between the two of you."

We looked at each other. General Shapiro could see we were worried.

"If it ain't broke, I say don't fix it." Monica started to get up from her chair. She hadn't wanted to go to Shapiro in the first place. It was I who'd insisted, realizing that our dwelling insurance premium would increase if our explosive sex continued to cause accidents for which we would have to file claims.

"You're afraid of change," he said. He was totally bald, but when he gave an insight, he brushed his hand along his scalp as if he still possessed hair. General Shapiro looked bereaved. He plainly regarded Monica's hesitancy about the treatment as an attack, and worse, an attempt to interrupt his chain of thought.

"How do you know what I am? You barely know me."

Shapiro and I looked at each other. In spite of Shapiro's dictatorial style it was also apparent that he made sense. Plainly, Monica was resistant.

"He's not saying we are going to lose all the fun we have, he's just saying we can make it better. We don't necessarily have to pay a price for pleasure. In this last instance, it was $1500 with the deductible!"

"Yes, and there is this other problem. What you're having is the equivalent of anonymous sex, of a succession of one-night stands." Shapiro was totally right, but even I wondered how he had been able to reach such definitive conclusions, considering how little chance he had given either Monica or I to complete a real patient interview.

"Excuse me, General Shapiro, but what right do you have to talk to us this way?" Monica said.

"Marty," he corrected.

"You're being crude. It's not professional."

"I'm trying to help."

"This way of talking isn't helping me."

"You two complain that your sex literally blows your minds. I'm trying to get you to see you can have wonderful sex without deleterious side effects."

I liked General Shapiro, but Monica couldn't stand his presumptuous manner. Shapiro and I both tried to explain that she was mistaking the messenger for the message. She said she hated him, but was it really him or what he was saying? I sagely nodded—as if I were somehow exempt from similar feelings— but I too was worried. We seemed to have the perfect chemistry. Why change a formula that had worked?

The reason became more apparent one night soon after our second meeting with Shapiro, when I was thrusting so hard into her that I actually broke a floorboard. The waterbed started to groan, and I knew if the bed broke its water again, the floor might buckle and even cave in. Monica, who was still alternately screaming out her usual, "Fuck me up the ass, oh, let me put my lips on your stinking hard joint motherfucker," and, "Where am I?" didn't understand when I slid out of bed, running for a huge roll of duct tape I kept around for just such emergencies. Luckily I had already dropped my load, and though my brains were fried, I had an uncharacteristic grip on reality due to my fear of our waterbed crashing onto the floor below. Isn't it amazing how challenging situations bring a person to his senses? As usual, Monica didn't remember anything. In fact, the only thing she said when I came up behind her in the bathroom as she was brushing her teeth before bed was, "Would you mind licking my asshole? I still have a little itch."

"We need to talk." How many times had I already invoked those words! We really didn't need to talk; it never did any good anyway, but I couldn't beat around the bush when human lives were at stake. Now we had a new problem on our hands because I had seen reality while Monica was still convinced that we could go on the way we were, without having any effect on others.

As the old saying goes, *it takes what it takes*, and it wasn't until we had done damage to the structure of the building that Monica was brought to her knees. She still didn't like Shapiro and continued to stonewall in our sessions, but she plainly needed him. Monica's one of those people who will never say she needs help, and she never admits she's gotten it, even when someone has been helpful. But the day the Department of Buildings got into the act and the big flatbeds pulled up with huge wooden beams that would be the new structure for one side of our building, Monica looked as if she was ready for anything. There was only one other tenant in the building besides the couple downstairs, an elderly woman who hadn't seen a prick in decades, and we all were put up in the local Motel 6 while the repairs were done. Anyone who'd lived in that building knew who the source of the trouble was. The young couple downstairs was understanding, but the elderly woman screamed at us in the most vile manner as we registered for our room.

"I did my share of fucking." She was waving her finger. "But you're a little cunt, miss. And you…" She pointed to me. "You seem like a very nice young man, but so was John Dillinger. You've got to put your dick back in your holster. Didn't the two of you ever hear of sublimation. I used to teach art history. Sublimation's when you take some of your sexual energies and turn them into art. Think of all the greatness that would lie ahead of you if you stopped trying to be the Black Stallion, young man. You're interested in theater sets. You could be the next Inigo Jones. And I wouldn't have to worry about the ceiling falling down every time I got into bed."

The first thing Shapiro asked us when we went to see him again was, "Are there things the two of you enjoy doing together besides sex?"

"That's how you think about things," Monica said. "If you're balanced you're good, if you're not balanced you're bad. It can only be one way. Well, we're not balanced. We have a wonderful relationship, but the only thing we like to do is fuck. We don't talk, we don't like gardening, we don't play tennis…." In spite of the damage to the structure of our building that'd been caused by our fucking, and the fact that she had appeared desperate at first, she still seemed to be intent on throwing a wrench into the couples counseling.

But then suddenly she grew quiet.

"What are you thinking?" Shapiro asked, running his hands through his non-existent hair. "Do you want to know what's striking from my perspective?"

"No."

"You see, that's striking too. First you're quiet, as if you want to listen. Then when I ask if you want help, you say no." Did Shapiro want to help or did he merely want to win? I wasn't sure, but I could tell he was having an effect.

୧

After several months in therapy, we began to see some improvement. There hadn't been any new structural damage to the building. On several occasions when the lack of new symptoms came up for discussion—at least the kind that were accompanied by building code violations—Shapiro asked coyly if we thought it had anything to do with the couples counseling. From Monica's perspective, Shapiro was more interested in proving he was right than in helping our relationship, and she had no intention of gratifying his wish by admitting he had done anything for us. In fact, I myself wasn't sure. Yes, it was true that no waterbeds had broken; yes, it was true that we were no longer looked at as a danger by our neighbors; yes, it was true there'd been no building inspectors knocking on our door at all hours of the day and night; no, we hadn't had to move into the Motel 6 any time lately. But the basic thing that held the fabric of our relationship together—the passionate, unforgiving fucking—was as intense as ever. We couldn't be together without fucking. One night we tried to follow Shapiro's advice and have a quiet candlelit dinner before jumping onto the waterbed, but we couldn't wait. We swept the cartons of moo shoo pork, fried rice, and crystal shrimp dumplings to the floor and made love right on the kitchen table. I felt I was following Shapiro's advice when I ate a few noodles off the table before sticking my face in Monica's spread legs, but the fact was, even the world's best lo mein was no competition for Monica's hairy cunt.

Monica continued to agree to see Shapiro because I claimed it was helping me. I was actually developing a good kind of self-consciousness when we fucked. Who wants to wake up to find out that when the moon came out he had turned into a werewolf and left a path of destruction in his wake? On the other hand, I never worried about Monica. She liked her sex rough. The more I stabbed at her, the further up her twat or asshole I penetrated, and the harder I did it, the happier she was. She also liked to be slapped around and spanked. Shapiro reassured us none of that had to change.

"No one is trying to malign your inventiveness, your athleticism, or your desire to make use of each other's every orifice," Shapiro stated, slamming a fist down on his desk. "But it's nice to feel you have choices. I don't sense you are choosing. It sounds like you are slaves to desire."

Despite the fact that Monica appreciated what Shapiro was doing for me, she was still resistant and resentful about seeing him. Everyone had to pay a price for their pleasures. A little bit of instability in the structure of a building didn't seem much of a sacrifice when it came to maximizing one's potential enjoyment of life. *If it ain't broke don't fix it* became Monica's mantra in counseling. The fact that we'd broken a dining room table, two sinks, a toilet seat, numerous waterbeds, and the beams holding up our downstairs neighbor's ceiling didn't faze her.

One morning Monica took my dick out of her mouth long enough to say, "We don't need couples counseling."

"What do you suggest then?" She put my dick back in her mouth, moving her thick lips up and down the shaft. She held her finger up in the air, motioning me to wait until she was done. Monica was actually competitive in her cock sucking. Each time she blew me, she wanted to see how much she could get in her mouth. But it wasn't in the least bit mechanical. She was exuberant. She licked and slurped like a child eating a fudgesicle on a hot day. She was aiming for the stem, a goal she'd never achieved without gagging, though she got closer every time she went down on me. Finally, just as she took my dick out, turning around so that I could put it in her ass, she said, "We just have to rent a first-floor apartment in a building with no basement. Then we won't have to worry about downstairs neighbors, beams...."

"Don't forget soundproofing." On several occasions, hearing Monica's screams, our neighbors had called the police. I wasn't being facetious when I told Monica, "We need to find one of those Nazi war criminals who built the torture chambers. They were experts on soundproofing. That's the only way we're going to feel free."

"Either that or we could move to the mountains."

"I don't mean this as a criticism honey, but the way you go on, we're liable to have hyenas and even bears scratching on our door."

Despite all the turmoil, each time Monica took her clothes off was a thrill for me. I gazed on Monica's pussy like a teenaged boy seeing a picture of a cunt in a dirty magazine for the first time. When she came out of the shower, I gloried in how much hair her Venus mound had. I loved the smell of her armpits, and when she walked by me in her underpants I wanted to pull them down and bury my face between her buttocks, as narrow, skinny, and tomboyish as they were. And I'm quite certain she felt the same way about me. Returning to Monica's body was like making a nostalgic visit back to the aunts and uncles who brought me up when my mother blew me off for not being a good enough fuck. They were of modest means; they never occupied mansions, but each room was filled with cherished memories of a boyhood characterized by sex fantasies and jerking off. Monica and I loved each other's bodies almost as much as we hated each other's minds. She hated couples counseling and my new-found concern for the sensibilities of our neighbors in the building, and I hated her stubborn refusal to realize that there were other things in the world besides fucking. Yet the two of us lived in the world. Some degree of control, of repression, was necessary even in the little society that was our relationship. Wasn't that, after all, what Freud was talking about in *Civilization and Its Discontents*?

Nevertheless, we both agreed we would be better off if we moved. We scanned the ads for ground-floor apartments. We found our dream villa, a reinforced concrete compound with only one small sound and shatterproof window that had originally been built as a fallout shelter. Apparently the original owners had built it above ground with the intention of finding the right underground resting place for it when it was completed. A pit would be dug and it would be lowered with steel cables. The fall of the Berlin Wall had intervened, and in lieu of its original use, it had gone on to have a glamorous history as a top secret government storage depot for germ warfare agents and, finally, as the arms storage hangar for the Brink's security company, before being rented to its first residential tenant. The bunker was in an industrial section of town. It was totally isolated—there wasn't another residence in a ten-block radius—but its fortified structure made it totally safe. We could fuck with all the abandon we had always wanted, without endangering the welfare of others. The moment we laid our eyes on the bare concrete walls and the space we wanted for the bedroom, which reminded us of the kind of deluxe cells reserved for Mafiosi in maximum security prisons, we knew we were on the road to attaining Nirvana.

I said goodbye to Shapiro. I liked him. He was my kind of person, a *no pain, no gain* kind of guy, but his in-your-face approach was not going to be successful in all instances. And with our concrete bunker, our "love garden," as we liked to call it, we wouldn't need to avail ourselves of his services. They say adversity makes for strange bedfellows, and I felt in the end that Monica developed a grudging admiration for Shapiro's tenacity and his continual willingness to help her, despite the way she both vociferously and taciturnly challenged his authority. Yes, by isolating ourselves from society in what was effectively a prison of our own making, we were treating the symptom rather than the problem. However, if you call savage fucking on a twenty-four hour basis a symptom, if you call a cunt as warm and salty as the Dead Sea and a dick as hard as the base of a coconut tree symptoms, if you call the screams and cries emanating from two humans of average consciousness and intelligence, sounding like dusk on the Zimbabwean veldt, a symptom, then these were the kinds of symptoms we didn't need to cure. Victimless crime has never qualified in my mind as a transgression. The drama of our lovemaking that played itself out on our enormous new waterbed every morning, evening, and afternoon (when I wasn't on the road)—a commotion that at the very least would have merited a quality-of-life violation in a normal neighborhood—was tacitly tolerated by the local authorities. If we didn't bother anyone, they wouldn't bother us. And who was there to bother—the hydraulic compactor next door, which slammed car parts into identical metal chunks with a ferocity that, hard as it is to believe, dwarfed my most fervent attempts at compacting Monica's private parts?

☙

Bill had gotten into a full-time aerobics certification program and he was having an affair with his instructor, which meant he could only sporadically cook for us. The single drawback to our new living quarters was the fact that we were so off the beaten track that many take-out places were reticent to deliver to our location. In particular a lot of the Chinese joints on which we depended weren't thrilled to fill our orders. Anyone who knows anything about the take-out business within our neck of the woods will tell you that it's divided up into neat little zones, and while we were only ten blocks from the nearest residential area, which was known universally as Chow (the one next to it was Mein), the blocks are long, and our place fell off to the edge of the neighborhoods outlined in colorful magic marker on the walls in the phone banks of the take-out joints. This meant that delivering Chinese food to us was essentially equivalent to delivering to another city.

In our town, Chinese food is a way of life; it's taken for granted like food stamps and other government subsidies. It's not so much a business as an aid program like CARE, that also happens to make a good profit for those who run it. Most people are dependent on Chinese food deliveries and would not be able to survive without them. So running a take-out route carries a certain level of social responsibility with it. The delivery boy working Chow never carries one order. When he goes out, he is feeding a whole area. Every time a take-out place conceded to take our order, they were in essence taking food out of the mouths of babes. At least these babes were going to have to wait long past their normal dinner hours to get their food.

We endured long periods when we weren't able to order in Chinese at all. Throughout the winter months, when the demand to satisfy the hungry mouths on the neighborhood routes is especially high, we didn't stand a chance. During these times we had to descend the food chain to Domino's Pizza and KFC, when we weren't lucky enough to receive shopping bags filled with little plastic containers—care packages from Bill. Monica and I could have gotten a wok and started to cook our own food, but then we would have had to shop. I worked hard when I was on a job, and when I came home at night I liked to fuck. In addition, as everyone knows, when it comes to Chinese food it's more expensive to cook it than to order it in.

Finally a solution arrived for our problem. It was a hot summer night. Many people in our part of the country still don't have air conditioning due to the expense and the fact that there are so few days when it really gets uncomfortable. But this was one of those brutal days. Most of town had been picnicking by the lake to stay out of the heat. The children could swim, and the adults could enjoy the breeze across the water, which creates little oases of coolness throughout even the warmest weather. We had our pick of take-out Chinese places since hardly anyone orders in during this kind of weather. I remember it well. I decided to try something different from the usual Number One: chicken chow mein, fried rice, egg roll, and wonton soup. I ordered wor shoo op, the braised duck dish I'd loved since I was a boy. It's a dish that's crunchy on the outside and soft inside, a little like Monica's cunt, whose large mound of hair you have to plow through to get to the juicy interior. Monica had the egg foo young combo, and she ordered egg drop soup, more because of the matching colors than because she liked the taste. We always fucked our brains out before we ordered in. We fucked our brains out after we ordered in too, for that matter. Anyway, I happened to be sitting on Monica's face when I noticed the delivery boy staring at us through the window. I waved and screamed out, "One minute."

"Look honey, the food's here, let me just come on your face."

"No," she whined. "I want to get fucked so bad." That's domesticity for you. In the throes of our first passion, Monica would have done anything I wanted, but now she was getting particular. It had to be a certain way or not at all. For instance, she liked to be fucked with one leg raised up in a stirrup she'd bought from a used obstetrical parts dealer. Every day it was something new. I knew the fucking was going to take longer than coming on her face, which was why I'd suggested the latter, but I also knew that on such a slow night, the delivery fellow wasn't going to get impatient and leave, as had happened on several other occasions when food arrived while we were in the middle of a drawn-out fuck. He'd need every tip he could get on a day like today.

When we were done, I rushed to the front door. I still had a hard-on—my hard-ons remained for over a half an hour after I fucked when I was really turned on—but it was rude enough keeping him as long as he'd already had to wait. I noticed right away that he didn't seem impatient at all. He seemed in a great mood in fact, and when I looked down, I noticed the gummy wet spot near his crotch which he'd neglected to wipe off. I guess he felt if we were letting it all hang out, he could too. His name was Ting, and he became our regular delivery person. I later learned that Ting was a refugee who had been forced to flee his native land because he was a member of the Falun Gong. I got so used to seeing his face at the window as Monica took my dick in her mouth, it was almost as if we were having a *ménage à trois*. We'd thought of inviting him in, but both of us agreed that the fun was in having someone looking at us. Anyway, Monica was afraid that, being a diminutive fellow, he'd probably have one of those skinny little cocks that she said look like dead mice. Needless to say, our problem with getting our take-out orders filled, in even the most inclement weather, was solved. We never went hungry again. We had blizzards, hurricanes, and even a tornado, but Ting was always there with our food, his beady eyes and flat impassive face pushed up against the window as I exploded my load into Monica's cunt, face, or ass.

Even though Monica couldn't bear the mention of General Shapiro's name, I often thought about the things he'd discussed with us. Shapiro had wanted to make it clear that modifying our behavior would not take anything away from us. In fact, it would increase our pleasures. And though we hadn't exactly followed his advice, I attributed our move to his sagacity. If we hadn't seen General Shapiro, we might have gone on fucking people out of their apartments; if it hadn't been a busted beam, it would have been a floorboard, or an overflowing bathtub (we couldn't get into the bathtub together without creating tempestuous currents and flooding—a man-made tropical storm that resulted in property damage that nearly rivaled the real thing). General Shapiro's advice made us look at our lives and take action. He was essentially saying *shit or get off the pot*. And we knew we had to get off the pot. But Shapiro was also trying to show us we didn't need to have such a narrow view of pleasure. There's fucking, and there are things like fucking when you don't explicitly fuck. Being in the arts world, I knew he was talking about sublimating sexuality into creative activities. But every time I said, "Let's do something like fucking, but not exactly fuck," Monica replied, "No... what're ya talking about?" By the time I started to explain that Shapiro wanted us to broaden our interests, Monica would already have my dick in her mouth—something that hastened the end of any conversation we might have had.

There's an old line from Freud, "Neurosis is reminiscence," which probably summarized the paralysis I was facing. I was stuck in repetitive behavior which derived from conflicts I'd always had with women. I didn't want to change anything in our lives, but I was troubled. One night after a particularly mind-blowing fuck, in which I was thrusting with such ferocity as Monica cried out for more that I thought the end of my dick was going to come out of her ass, I found myself wandering in the neighborhood just as in the old days. For a moment I didn't know who I was or where. No one had ever bothered us in our industrial neighborhood, and at night the streets could be quite empty. On this occasion, I was confronted by two oversized gentlemen who called me a "punker" and started to punch me in the head. Seeing me staggering and disoriented after the fuck, the two bullies probably thought I was on something. Speaking of reminiscence, I had a feeling of déjà vu.

"I'm not a punker. Punk has been dead for decades anyway," I cried as I fell to the pavement. My attacker showed his appreciation for the historical correction by kicking me in the head.

I was knocked unconscious as I had been that first night I met Bill. It was all just a weird coincidence. Once again, when I awakened I couldn't move my arm. I'd dislocated my shoulder.

However, in terms of knowing what was going on, I was in better shape this time. I called Monica. Of course, on the way to the hospital in the ambulance, Monica insisted that sucking my dick would be the best way to alleviate the pain.

In the aftermath of a traumatic event, the victim tends to feel totally helpless. I was imprisoned by my sling and the mixture of pain and paralysis I faced whenever I tried to take the arm out. How would I mount Monica with my arm in this condition? How would she be able to climb on top of me? But all human beings are entrepreneurs at heart, and the ability of the individual to use invention to counteract adversity is almost endless. You have only to look at the ways in which humans have adapted to the exigencies of eccentric environmental and topographical challenges. Look at Mont St. Michel! Within the confines of the hospital, where I also recovered from a concussion and a broken finger, we came up with positions we had never tried before. My injury had unleashed the childlike propensity to play that lurks deep down inside all of us. Rather than bemoaning the loss of my arm, I actually began to enjoy the limitations that had been imposed on me by illness. Monica and I became deeply involved in toe sucking, which is also known as shrimping. At one point, as she stood over my face, looking down at me imperiously with stiletto heels, a leather bustier, and nothing else on, I actually thanked my assailant aloud. I was silenced from continuing with my encomium to his ability to maim when Monica took off her shoe and shoved her big toe into my mouth. She'd just gotten a pedicure, and the alcohol smell of nail polish mixing with the herring scent of pussy is an aroma I will always connect with room 810 in Central General Hospital.

How reticent we are to break the rigid routines which dominate our existence! Strange as it may seem, getting mugged opened my eyes up to some aspects of Monica I'd never seen before. Normally, I mounted her from her right side, so I got a good view of her right arm and shoulder. When it came to caressing, I paid more attention to her right breast because I was there first, and I used her right shoulder to catapult myself on top of her. Now with my left side immobilized, I had to start to mount her by pushing off with my right arm, thus favoring her left shoulder, arm, and breast. I'd never noticed it. Her left nipple was slightly larger then her right. Isn't it strange that you think you know a person, and it's only under conditions of great stress—like soldiers under fire—that you *really* come to know each other? The time I spent in Central General was a journey of discovery. In two days, Monica and I discovered what General Shapiro had been unsuccessfully trying to show us for months—that pleasure was an open door rather than a set of rigid rules. During my first day, I was in great discomfort. There were a few times when Monica wanted to fuck that I couldn't rise to the occasion. I was in so much pain that I didn't even want a blowjob. Monica started to tell me stories to relax me and hopefully to lull me to sleep. The stories, of course, reflected her preoccupations. They were all about stud-like princes with enormous cocks, and horny maidens who wanted to get fucked in the ass by the stud-like prince and all his friends. There were romantic moonlight gangbangs on deserted beaches and tales of lonely beauties on windswept heaths with only their trusty stallions to blow. At one point, as my eyes closed and Monica's tale spread itself out before my imagination, I felt myself starting to come without her even touching me. I look back on this as a white-light experience, a moment of spiritual enlightenment I wouldn't have had if it weren't for the brutal beating I took.

Just two days after we returned home from the hospital, I noticed the first real change in our relationship. I'd had to fly out of town for a one-day consultancy on a production of *The Pajama Game* opening in Dubuque. When I returned home that night, we were back to our usual selves. Monica had already ordered my egg roll. Ting had his nose up against the window, and Monica had her mouth tightly wrapped around my cock. As she knelt down in front of me and started to lick under my balls, making her way up the chocolate brick road, I noticed Ting's hand moving up and down. It was all reassuringly the same. What was wonderful about our relationship was our ability to do the same things all the time while getting ever greater enjoyment from them. Our ability to squeeze so much pleasure out of similar circumstances was a primitive expression of gratitude, I suppose. I thought to myself that nobody had ever sucked my cock and licked my asshole the way Monica could. I loved her technique as much as I loved her; in fact, I'd come to understand that it was her sexual technique that was the heart of my love for her.

We paid Ting after the first fuck. That way we knew all three of us were satisfied. Before eating, we'd have a second fuck. It was after the second fuck—often the most powerful in that it made me ejaculate from the very core of my being—that she popped out with a question that had never crossed her lips before. "Could we go to the museum?" she asked as she got up to dip my egg roll in mustard before thrusting it in my mouth. General Shapiro's advice had finally penetrated her defenses.

She was speaking of our local municipal museum, which has had the same exhibit of American Indian blankets for the past quarter of a century. Considering the generally low level of social services in our area and the glaring need for things like road repair, arts funding has never been a priority. I'd done a few plays at our local regional theater, but stopped when they got a director who was a John Phillip Sousa nut; the past two seasons had been totally devoted to a thirty-hour-long tribute to Sousa that made *Der Ring des Nibelungen* look like an episode of "Barney," and our one opera house rarely deviates from Gilbert and Sullivan. Despite the fact I don't have the slightest interest in Indian blankets, I considered Monica's suggestion. Maybe it was just age. Time tames even the wildest stallions. Even the toughest neo-Nazi biker, who has spent half his life behind bars, starts to think about retirement communities once he gets out of jail and stops having to worry about former enemies coming up behind him with a piece of wire. Maybe Monica was ready to settle down.

However, I had to ask myself, did I really want to encourage her? I may have started the ball rolling by dragging her to Shapiro, but did I want to suffer the consequences? Wouldn't we disagree about the Indian blankets just as we had about other subjects on the few occasions we had talked in the past? Monica was a great fuck. Everyone grows old and dies, and someday I'd have to deal with that, but why not enjoy it for today and worry later about what kind of rapport we'd have once our life of ferocious fucking and sucking was over.

I wasn't going to introduce something new into our routine just to take up Monica's dare. I'm not a chance-taker at heart. I've always liked getting laid, but I'm not the kind of guy who makes a grandstand play, swinging from the nearest vine like Tarzan to get the good-looking girl. In fact, it's amazing I've gotten fucked and sucked as much as I have.

Yet somehow I knew General Shapiro made sense. You didn't order in Chinese every day because of the cuisine. It wasn't that I just liked sticking my joint in Monica's hot honey pot; I didn't like anything else anymore. Cooking, which had once been an interest, was swept under the table by the sex. Good music, books, cinema and, yes, art were all falling by the wayside because of our addiction to each other's bodies. I was living proof that when you don't employ a given human capacity, it atrophies. I picked up our local version of *Time Out*, a paper called *What's Going On In Town*. The museum was open on Tuesday, Wednesday, and Thursday from ten until five and on

Fridays and Saturdays from ten until eight forty-five.

"If we go on Friday at five we can get home in time to order in and fuck." I was trying to be practical. There's no sense in making culture a matter of punishment and deprivation; that takes away from its potential to be a source of pleasure. I remembered sitting through an all-female production of *Henry IV Part II* in Paris, Kentucky, in which the part of Prince Hal was played by a recovering sex addict who had just gotten out of rehab. The lines, spoken in a thick Southern drawl, all sounded like a waitress asking if you wanted a refill on your coffee. My need to sit through the entire performance was just the kind of compulsiveness I wanted to spare Monica. I didn't want her feeling that going to the museum was a chore or duty or something that had to be done unremittingly in order to achieve some required level of perfection.

"We're going to have to push our late-afternoon fuck back to four."

"If we go on Thursday at four we end up killing our late afternoon fuck. Then we get home too early for our evening fuck. So we have a fuck that's neither fish nor fowl."

"Is there any possibility we could have one of our fucks while we're there and another when we get home?"

"General Shapiro wanted us to try something different."

"That's why I'm suggesting it. If this art thing is a substitute for sex, it's going to turn me on." I didn't pay attention to the warning. It seemed ridiculous to be phobic about art.

૭

You've probably guessed it. Monica became as addicted to art as she was to sex. The notion she could miss any exhibit was an affront. After the Indian quilts, there was the traveling show of Flemish floral design drawings and the etchings by someone who identified herself as Charles Manson's aunt—a show she forced me to fly to Detroit to see the day it opened. We started to travel around the country to see art shows, a practice that tied in nicely with my career in the musical theater. I'd been scheduled to work on an *Annie* in Akron. Monica arrived on a Monday a few days after the rehearsals began. Monday is the one day you have off in a rehearsal period, and for the first time I could see that Monica was torn. When I looked into her eyes I knew she wanted to fuck, the way I know a python likes to eat live rabbits. Usually she'd have my fly open and my dick in her mouth before we'd even said a word to each other, but this time she managed to get out, "I want to see the Anaïs Nin…." The rest of her sentence was muffled by the suction of her lips against the shaft of my prick, although any good cryptographer could have made out what she was talking about. Through the muffled sounds and groans I managed to get the idea that Monica wanted to see an exhibit of Anaïs Nin's letters displayed on the first floor of the Akron Museum of Modern Art.

During the reading of an exchange between Anaïs Nin and Henry Miller, Monica briefly lost control. You hear about elderly people who lose control of their bowels and bladder. Our little visit to the show at the Akron should have warned me. I don't think even a genius like General Shapiro could have predicted the effect art would have on Monica. Rather than helping her to sublimate her sexual instincts, art seemed to flood her, if it's possible to imagine, with even higher levels of sexual passion. It's lucky the Akron Museum of Modern Art has few visitors and in fact, relatively few works of art. Monica got down on all fours and demanded I fuck her like a dog in the middle of the gallery. The Akron's one female guard turned away when she saw what was transpiring. When you run an exhibit of writing by Anaïs and Henry Miller, you expect anomalous behavior, but this wouldn't be the last time art would have an explosive effect on Monica's sexuality. I looked Monica's symptoms up on the internet. Her symptoms would later evolve into something more complex, for which General Shapiro would eventually offer a different diagnosis, but at this point it seemed to me she had contracted a condition called Maecenatism, in which patients suffer from uncontrollable sexual urges when they look at paintings and other creative works. The condition is also referred to in the literature as "negative sublimation." In normal sublimation, erotic energy is turned into art. The negative form presents the reverse scenario. Art is turned back into the erotic energy that initially fueled its creation.

I liked going to museums and seeing paintings, but my reactions fell more into the realm of the kind of modulated behavior that General Shapiro was trying to lead the two of us towards. I genuinely found walking around museums with Monica to be a satisfying, relaxing new way of channeling my often anarchic and errant sexual desires—that is, for the first few moments we were together. After that, the associations became too powerful for Monica and she couldn't stop herself. I was so turned on by her being turned on that I became her inadvertent accomplice. Most museums are filled with signs that warn, "Please do not touch the works of art." At the Boise Center for Contemporary American Painting, Monica pinned me up against an erotic painting by Eric Fischl, and a show of Jackson Pollock's action paintings at the Wadsworth in Schenectady stimulated Monica to look for action, which in this case meant straddling me in the first stall of the gallery's bathroom.

When I had to go to Manhattan to meet with the agency that gets me my gigs in the musical theater, we stopped off at the Metropolitan Museum of Art. Monica had by this time become addicted to modernism. She was as addicted to modernism as she was to sex and was as desperate about modernism (and sex for that matter) as any crack or heroine addict is for drugs. Abstract expressionism was particularly a problem for her. The dripping techniques and the emphasis on action obviously touched those parts of the brain that generate feelings of pleasure—and the prospect of seeing Jackson Pollock's *Autumn Rhythm*, an enormous paint-spattered canvas, sent her into a complete paroxysm of desire. As we walked up the huge central staircase to the second floor, she started to grab at my testicles. Then she dug her hand into my pants. As I've said, all I need is for Monica to be in the vicinity. I can get a hard-on just having her near, but when she fondles my dick and balls and sticks her finger up my ass as she did when we approached the last few steps, my crotch begins to look like a spacious tent on a camp site. The sight of the actual painting, with its streak of yellow, made her whisper urgently, "You've got to do it to me right here, right now."

"What?"

She opened her mouth wide.

"Pee."

She dragged me by the hand. There's a little garden in back of the museum, and in front of a group of horrified mothers who covered their children's eyes, Monica got down on her knees and demanded I splatter her face with urine, the way Jackson Pollock had splattered his canvases with paint.

Sometimes you try to help people with their addictions by encouraging abstention or by just letting them wear themselves out. However, when Monica wanted something, a team of wild horses was not going to stop her. Threatening to abstain from sex with her was not going to work. She knew I couldn't resist her, and all I can say is not a day went by without some new paraphilia appearing in our sex lives. As far as sex was concerned, I knew there was nothing I could do to make her amend her behavior. So rather than trying to prevent her from acting out, I became her enabler. I decided to give her as much of the mixture of abstract expressionism and unbridled sexuality as she wanted, in the hope that one day she would reach what in the recovery movement they call "a bottom." A bottom is a low point; some people lose all their friends, some people get sick, some have a near-death experience. I was going to have to lie back and enjoy Monica's descent because base camp was nowhere in sight.

At one point, Monica jerked me off on a painting by the Japanese minimalist, Yoshi Yokoshida, that was showing in a gallery in Providence. We were about to be booked on a charge of desecrating private property when Yokoshida, in town for a retrospective, intervened on our behalf. We were released when he told the police my ejaculations were a serendipitous addition to his work. The experience, however, left an indelible impression on my mind. After having sex on or near a number of De Koonings, Rothkos, Nolands, a Kandinsky, and several Rauschenbergs, I had a new idea. "You know, honey, there are lots of starving artists who would be willing to have you roll all over their freshly painted canvases if you paid them a few bucks…."

"Do you think they would take money? Don't you think they would regard that as selling out?"

"They wouldn't feel they were selling out taking money for you to roll naked in acrylics. For them it would just be another experience—perhaps even a source of inspiration for new work."

As everyone knows, Soho, the former home of New York's art world, has been turned into a gigantic shopping mall that rivals the best that New Jersey has to offer in terms of barren commercialism. Most of the starving artists now live in the Williamsburg section of Brooklyn, and it was there that we made the acquaintance of the brothers Ivan and Dimitri Lermontov. They weren't exactly abstract expressionists. Being Russian, they had a nostalgia for the early years after the Russian Revolution and before the advent of Stalin, when the esthetic and political avant-gardes were in sync. They loved the geometry of the Constructivists and Malevich and evinced their obsession with the square, for example, by doing renderings of linoleum floors. Still, they had no problem with Monica and me fucking our brains out on their huge freshly painted canvases. They didn't even ask for money. Even though they were inspired by an altogether different movement, they subscribed to the abstract expressionist idea that the painting was a memento of an act that once occurred. Instead of money they wanted the right to exhibit what they called "the remembrances of things past." They wanted to immortalize our modernist fucks, and we weren't averse to being their *Davids*.

At first I had a little trouble convincing Monica. Ivan and Dimitri weren't pure abstract expressionists. It was a little like trying to give coke to a methamphetamine addict. But once she got used to the feel of rolling in their paints, she wouldn't have her art sex any other way. This was our real introduction to the heyday of the Russian avant-garde. Monica never had much interest in words, but I became interested in a few of the poets of the era—in particular, Mayakovsky, who was a great favorite of the Lermontov brothers. The age of Russian artistic freedom was short-lived, however, and Stalinist socialist realism ushered in an era of artistic repression.

If our energies had been confined to fucking our brains out on the Lermontov's canvases, we wouldn't have had a problem. It was what occurred when we had finished working with the brothers that bothered me. Our couplings in Williamsburg were the most memorable of our whole relationship, but instead of satiating us, they made us want more and more. I was beginning to feel my years. After fucking Monica up the ass on a succession of white squares reminiscent of Malevich's *White on White*, I could have gone home and watched some television. But Monica, the instigator, kept seeking out higher levels of pleasure, and I was never able to resist her scent.

The art-world sex was like a powerful chain reaction that couldn't be stopped. Even though we always got the last two seats at the back of the plane on our trips home, we still ran into trouble. The only thing you're explicitly not allowed to have in your mouth on an airplane is a cigarette, but most airlines don't look kindly on blowjobs, even if they're done underneath a blanket. The sight of Monica's bobbing head and my mouth stuffed with her fingers to muffle my cries, resulted in some tense exchanges with the cockpit.

General Shapiro had created a monster. After one of our trips—I don't remember which; the past has become a blur of canvas, acrylic paint, and cunt in my mind—I came home determined to do something about our relationship. Monica might not have reached her bottom, but I had. After all, I was a man of the theater. I had a professional identity for which it was important to maintain at least a veneer of respectability. I still considered myself a member of society. What had happened in our apartment building was happening all over again. Our sex was resulting in our being ostracized. I could have pointed my finger at the repression of American society; I could have said it was like the Salem Witch hunts, or the McCarthy trials; I could have compared Monica and me to the Hollywood Ten; I could have looked at Monica as an Alger Hiss-type martyr, but I realized that—when an eight-year-old flying on the same flight cries out, "Mommy, why does that lady have a penis in her mouth?"—it was Monica and I who had to change.

I knew we never should have quit Shapiro in the first place. The cement bunker was only a band-aid. It had been a wonderful solution, but it wasn't going to solve all our problems. You can't live in a state of total soundproof isolation, and you can't live on a total Chinese take-out diet. In addition, I'm basically a social creature. I need more than the leering eyes of a Chinese delivery boy for friendship. How was I going to get us back into treatment? As far as Monica was concerned, she was happy. My plan of enabling her and letting her spiral to a bottom had obviously backfired. She was more addicted than ever. I wasn't going to be able to conquer such a problem on my own. I needed a power greater than myself. I needed General Shapiro, but Monica wasn't going to take kindly to an intervention—especially one performed by Shapiro, whose crude methods and blunt truths she still claimed to despise. Shapiro was also a bit of a prima donna. You don't get to be the highest-ranking Jewish marriage counselor in the history of the United States Army without having run the gauntlet. Shapiro's climb up the ladder of the military couples counseling establishment had obviously hardened him, but also made him cranky and erratic at times. Who knew what would happen when I called to ask for help? He'd promised he would see us anytime we needed him, but finding an available hour with someone whose time was so coveted would not be easy. He'd have us over a barrel. He'd find the hour, but it would be a sacrifice on his part and he'd let us know it. There was going to be pressure on Monica to change, and Monica didn't respond well to coercion.

I wasn't looking forward to seeing the sneer that always crossed Monica's face when I mentioned Shapiro's name, nor was I looking forward to the stream of invective that would pour out of her mouth. She had nothing nice to say about the man, although in her more contemplative moments she admitted he'd helped us. After all, she wouldn't have become addicted to abstract expressionism if it weren't for him, and she wouldn't have attained a state of orgasm that made tantric sex look like Puritan love at Plymouth Rock.

One day I took the plunge. It was somewhere between our second and third fuck, so it must have still been early morning when I snuck off into the kitchen and picked up the phone.

Monica was in her usual state of post-coital delirium. I could hear her moaning, "Fuck me, fuck me, fuck me," from our bedroom. The abandon that had characterized my earliest days with her had long passed. I'd become so concerned about the wake of destruction that followed our sexual escapades that I was rarely if ever *non compos mentis* after sex anymore. I got General Shapiro's answering machine message. *This is Doctor Shapiro on an answering machine. Please leave your name, number, and the time you called, and I will get back to you shortly.* Shapiro had grown up on the wrong side of the tracks; there was a pugnacity in the tone of the message that went back to his hardscrabble childhood. His voice echoed as if he were booming out a message to his troops in some chilly airplane hangar along the 38th parallel in Korea.

I hesitated for a moment as the tape ran.

"General Shapiro, hi… it's James Moran. Um, let's see, I'd like to talk to you about Monica and myself, but at this point I would rather you didn't call me at home."

"Hi, Mr. Moran, it's Dr. Shapiro." The echoing sound in the background of the answering machine message was still there even though the message itself had stopped. Did he dictate his message in some dank cave? Did this tough veteran of sexual warfare inhabit some rugged mountain lair when not in his office?

"I think a complication has set in. It's like when you get an infection after surgery. That suggestion about getting interested in other things besides sex is where it all started."

"I know. She's got *hypergraphia satyriasis*."

"Don't you want to hear what she's been doing?"

"I know, I know…."

"She got interested in abstract expressionism, but it only increased her desires. We're getting thrown out of museums, office buildings—anywhere there's public art poses a problem." I blurted out her symptoms as fast as I could. When General

Shapiro made his mind up about a diagnosis, nothing would shake him, and even though many of his diagnoses had nothing to do with any symptoms we described, he always seemed to hit the nail right on the head. *Hypergraphia satyriasis* sounded right, though hypergraphia referred to the compulsion to write, and satyriasis was a sexual compulsion restricted to men. You had to take Shapiro with a grain of salt, or you wouldn't get anything out of him at all. For all I knew, the diagnosis could have referred to the case of another patient, but it didn't matter. As Shapiro had pointed out, he rarely experienced any failure in his many years of work. So even if he was treating Monica for the wrong ailment, he'd undoubtedly come up with the right cure.

"It's the *hypergraphia satyriasis.* She's a *hypergraphic.* She's not suffering from cancer. *Hypergraphics* go on to live totally normal lives."

"I'm not doubting your diagnosis, but what do we do if she rejects it. It's unfortunate, but you are providing her with grist for her mill. She finds you totally irresponsible in these diagnoses, and here you come up with an ailment whose chief symptom, compulsive writing, has nothing to do with her. Then to make matters worse, you make up a dual diagnosis giving her a second ailment that primarily afflicts males."

"It's not a dual diagnosis. If you look in the DSM, *hypergraphia satyriasis* is listed. She has an anomalous form of it that derives from the same source. The same neuronal structures in the brain are affected, only in Monica's case the symptom is compulsive sexuality in the presence of abstract paintings rather than compulsive writing of dirty novels, which is the actual everyday manifestations of the *hypergraphia* in typical cases. In an atypical case like Monica's, you have a permutation. The abstract expressionist lines are like scribble. The pornography usually confined to the page takes place on or near canvases, but I don't think we're far off the mark. Psychopharmacologists medicate *hypergraphics*, but I don't think Monica needs medication. Monica is afraid of being happy. It causes her anxiety. This sexuality is just her way of avoiding pleasure." I couldn't see him, but I was sure that Shapiro was running his fingers through his non-existent hair.

"We've used our bodies to have out-of-body experiences. The intensity of our sexuality has alienated us from our selves."

Shapiro sighed. He was bored. He hated it when patients talked about their problems. He especially hated it when patients offered diagnoses that differed from his own. The tone of his voice said *fine, think whatever you want, but don't tell me*. My analysis was not as long as Shapiro's, but I thought brilliant. Shapiro was like my father. He never paid any attention to anything I said. That's why I ended up fucking my mother. Out of body *body* experience; I couldn't believe Shapiro didn't realize my brilliance, but I wasn't surprised. If he acknowledged me then he wouldn't be able to take all the credit for the cure. Shapiro was like a hunter who stuffs the carcasses of his prey and hangs them on his trophy wall. He wanted Monica's tusk. If someone was going to get better in his office, Shapiro made sure it was his fault.

Before we got off the phone, Shapiro issued an ultimatum. Either we came three days a week, or he wouldn't see us at all.

"Why three? I've never heard of anybody going three times a week to couples counseling."

"We're not talking about anybody. We're talking about you. It's like Monica claiming that there's nothing wrong with your relationship since everyone else you know fucks their brains out and has to move into concrete bunkers to protect neighbors. Anyway, we know what one day a week did. You guys are the living proof that a little knowledge can be a dangerous thing. You need a lot of knowledge." He laughed heartily at his own joke.

I had to think. Monica was lying on the bed rocking from side to side in that way she did when she was still horny. I fucked her one more time. All of our fucks tended to be astounding, but this was a particularly good one. I was as hard as one of those impenetrable metal alloys they talk about in the safe-making business. I was so hard that we ended up in what we call "lockdown." I had trouble getting it out of her. After I was done I had one of my old-fashioned out-of-body moments. I didn't know who or where I was. I came to in the same pizzeria I'd gone to the day I met Bill. Despite the decision that lay before me, I felt pretty fulfilled. I was getting laid more than I ever had, and it wasn't in order to prove myself. I'd never been in a situation where I wanted to fuck and had my desires so readily reciprocated. I'd been with women who wanted to fuck me when I had little interest in them, and I'd been with many women whom I wanted to fuck, who never seemed to feel like it. Finally, I'd met a soul mate. Yes, we needed change, but I didn't want to throw the baby out with the bath water.

After the pizza I stopped off in a bar. There's nothing like an ice-cold beer when you've got to think things over. I had one, then another one, and another one. I started to feel bold and sure of myself. I was going to walk in the door, fuck Monica one more time, and read her the riot act. Those beers really made me feel powerful. No one was going to push me around—not Monica, not even General Shapiro. I was fearless. I continued ordering beers. All I wanted to do was drink and continue with my wonderful fantasies about what a big shot I was. Why should I bother going home and fighting it out when I could sit at the bar and have these wonderful feelings? I didn't need anyone. I was free.

"I'm drunk. Now we have a real old-fashioned couples counseling problem," I screamed, as a whiskey with a beer chaser sent me out on the street where I could tell my tale to the world. I could spot several people looking out their windows to see what the commotion was all about.

"And I wonder how Monica and Shapiro are going to handle it," I continued.

"Hey buddy, people are trying to sleep," someone yelled out the window.

"Sleep it off, you bum!" Now I had a real audience. I've always loved theater; fortified by the drink, I proceeded to give a performance that equaled Ray Milland in *Lost Weekend* (1945) or Jack Lemmon in *Days of Wine and Roses* (1962).

Luckily I made my way back to the bunker, but when I stumbled in, Monica was furious. I started to whistle the old disco song "I Like the Night Life."

"You smell like you've been drinking."

"I have to talk to you about something." I was slurring my words. "Shapiro thinks we have to see him three times a week."

She went into the bathroom and slammed the door. Was this what it had come to? After traveling around the country to gratify Monica's need to fuck in the presence of abstract expressionist masterpieces, I was getting slapped on the wrist for a night of profligacy. The injustice made me want to drink.

"My father was a drinker," she said as she emerged several minutes later. She'd calmed down; her initial repulsion was gone. She'd obviously been giving my drinking some thought; her tone was rational and forgiving.

She immediately pulled up her skirt and sat on my prick, which was instantaneously hard despite the condition of the rest of my body. "And when he was drunk he always made me blow him. But I've been thinking about my art history. Jackson Pollock also liked to drink. In fact, he crashed his car into a telephone pole and died because he was DWI."

The therapeutic effects of a good fuck never ceased to amaze me. As Monica bobbed on top of me, my wooziness disappeared. I felt as if I'd undergone an exorcism. Plainly, the legendary drinking of the abstract expressionists had validated my drunken episode for Monica. Not only did it no longer disgust her, she was finding my alcoholism to be a turn-on.

I owed Shapiro a call. After all, he'd been of help. But besides calling Shapiro, I also had to start attending AA meetings. I'd only been drinking for 24 hours, but it was a day-at-a-time program, and my brief experience told me that booze had me by the balls. I was headed down a road of self-destruction that would make the busted waterbeds and fractured beams Monica and I had caused in our search for sexual oblivion seem like child's play.

I bit the bullet and phoned Shapiro again. I knew I would get his answering machine, and I'd come to enjoy listening to his message as much as I liked speaking to him. *This is Doctor Shapiro on an answering machine. Please leave your name, number, and the time you called, and I will get back to you shortly.* In its blunt drawl and its emphasis on the word *answering machine*, it exemplified everything Shapiro was about. It was obvious an answering machine was picking up, but he needed to state the obvious anyway.

"Hi, Doctor Shapiro, it's James Moran. Say, I haven't really had the chance to discuss the three days a week with Monica because we've been tied up." Yes, if you call drinking oneself into oblivion and fucking your brains out being tied up. And no, if you mean being tied up like some of the guys in The Golden Cock were tied up. "Look, if it's okay with you, I think the two of us need to come in to discuss the three-days-a-week idea in person."

ℭℨ

I'll never forget my first AA meeting. The meeting was held in the basement of a church, and when the chairman asked, "Is there anyone attending an AA meeting for the first time—this is not to embarrass you, but to welcome you," I cautiously raised my hand and said, "I'm James—actually it's Jim." *Yes, I was Jim, not James. How many years had I hidden behind James? I was a Jim, just another Jim like other guys were Johns, not some hoity toity James, a name that begged for an honorific.* Having made this crucial decision, my voice became firm, strong, and decisive. "I'm Jim. I'm an alcoholic, and this is my first time at an AA meeting."

My first few meetings were really rough. I hated the constant repetitions of how grateful everyone was for being in the program. Sometimes newcomers like myself would arrive at the meeting and totally break down, crying about how they hated their marriages, their jobs, their children. These outbursts were met with the chant "keep coming back." The seemingly positive-sounding "keep coming back," I would later learn, is the AA equivalent of an insult. Yes, it's nice to know you're wanted, yet when you're told to "keep coming back," it means you're wanted not for your knowledge, your wit, your intelligence, or your understanding; it means "keep coming back" because you don't know anything and you're an accident waiting to happen. Even though I didn't have too many meltdowns during my first meetings, I wasn't safe from the "keep coming back" crowd who told me to "keep coming back" every time I shared.

Like many close relatives of alcoholics, Monica had as much trouble with me being in the program as she'd had during the one day I was a raging alcoholic. In her case the normal problems of adapting to your partner being involved in a totally new world was complicated by the fact that she had come to like the idea I was an alcoholic. She didn't just like it, she was enthralled by it. The disgust she had initially felt disappeared when she realized that my disheveled appearance reminded her of De Kooning. Not only was she competing with my new program friends for affection and attention, she resented the program's results. She actually wanted me to come home smelling like a brewery. Now, seeing me in a sober state, talking about my feelings instead of acting out, made her feel uncomfortable. Sobriety can be as much a threat as active alcoholism, and that is what seemed to be occurring in our case. In order to make myself attractive to Monica again, I didn't want to do things that were bad for my body. When, after returning home from a meeting one night, I soberly asked Monica if we could go in to Shapiro for a consultation, to my surprise she said, "You better do it," which was her way of saying we needed help.

I had never expected to find myself in General Shapiro's office again. Shapiro kept pictures of all the couples he'd helped on the wall, the way hunters preserve their conquests. He even had a trophy case which displayed the many awards he'd received. He'd won the Interborough Best Couples Therapist Citation in 1971 and '72 consecutively, and he had runner-up ribbons for 1974 and 1978. He either stopped competing or training from the late '70s until the mid '80s because the next trophy was third place in the nationals, which he received in 1986, and which solidified his status. When Shapiro referred to himself as a world-class marriage counselor, this was obviously the period he was talking about. He'd entered the metros throughout the early '90s, receiving all sorts of awards, but after that, there was nothing. I suppose after all the years in Vietnam and then on the couples counseling circuit, Shapiro, like a fighter past his prime, had finally hung up his gloves—at least as far as the competitive couples counseling circuit was concerned. Still, as he frequently had reminded us, he only wanted to help.

"Do you *really* want to help us, or to show us how much you know?" Monica had asked some months before, at the end of what we thought would be our last session.

"Isn't it interesting how every time I offer to help, you try to figure out some evil motive?"

"I'm not saying you're evil; you're just like the rest of us."

"Out for myself, eh." And that's how we had left it. We were back again, and there was a surreal quality to it all. Shapiro looked as if he had aged, and I wondered now as I had in the past if the frustration of working with us was actually bad for his health. Shapiro liked helping people, but even more than helping he liked the feeling of success. And while I didn't aspire to join the gallery of legendary patients hanging from his wall, I didn't like seeing a gallant warrior like General Shapiro, whose office had been a war zone, crashing up against the shoals of a comparatively innocuous case. For a man who brought together husbands and wives whose jobs literally required them to try to kill each other during the working day, our case should have been child's play, but it wasn't. I knew we had become the mountain Shapiro sought to climb. We were his great white whale, his *Moby Dick*.

"I told James that I would be happy to see you folks," Shapiro began. "But I won't see you unless you agree to come three times a week."

"Nobody goes to couples counseling three times a week."

"Yes, and according to you nobody has a relationship in which they have very occasional and unmemorable sex."

"I told you, most people I know like to fuck and suck and get fucked in the ass. As someone who is proud of the cum on her face, I'd say that every sexual event is like the eruption of Mount Vesuvius. It has historical importance, if you know what I mean."

"I was trying to show you a different way of looking at things."

"Yeah, and you made it worse. Now sex is better, but it's more complicated because of the museums. Even that picture on your wall is turning me on." It was a reproduction poster of a 1952 Matisse exhibit at the Gallerie Maeght in Paris. "I'd say three days a week, and we're going to have to hold on for dear life. All we need is one more art appreciation tip...."

"Can I make a suggestion?"

Monica didn't say anything; nothing she said would have stopped him anyway.

"Can I suggest that you stop looking at art for a while?"

"But you were so sure, so positive and insistent."

"Therapists try different hats on to see if the right one fits." Since General Shapiro was totally bald, he didn't need to try on different hats; his head size was a constant that could easily be measured. Shapiro reached over to get his appointment book. The hunter had his prey. Shapiro's nostrils curled up. He'd finally snagged his two most elusive prizes. Before we knew it he'd have us skinned, stuffed, and mounted on the wall. I knew Monica couldn't bear the thought of all the pleasure General Shapiro was going to get from *helping us*. We were getting fucked by him. You would have thought that someone who loved fucking as much as Monica did would have enjoyed it. But she liked to choose her partners. This was rape.

"I'm very busy. There are lots of openings in Milwaukee, Akron, Toledo, Dayton," Monica said dismissively.

"I thought we were talking about putting art on the backburner," Shapiro countered.

Monica emitted a horrible cackle that sounded like a death rattle. She had many horrible traits, but this expression of her disgust with Shapiro made my blood curdle. "*We* never said anything. You said it." We were back to step one with Monica finding fault with anything General Shapiro tried to say. Monica had an ability to dissect a person's sentences that would have made her the envy of even the most gifted analytic philosophers. The problem was that she had spent so much of her adult life fucking, she had had little time to develop a well-rounded intellect to match. And most of her comments were about as helpful to a therapeutic encounter as a slasher is to a street whore.

 CS

The weeks that followed weren't any more productive. I was earnestly trying to deal with my alcoholism, but Monica seemed more intent on correcting General Shapiro's therapeutic methods than in getting help with the *hypergraphia satyriasis* that had ravaged her body. When you get so worked-up by abstract expressionist painting, you pay a price. In Monica's case, though the ailment had affected her physically (by making her supernaturally horny), the deleterious results were mostly emotional. Monica was going through a stage where she mounted me whenever I was lying down. We didn't have to be in the vicinity of an artwork. The stimulation of the gallery visits spilled over from one day to the next. Her compulsion was so strong that I felt she didn't even know I was there, and it brought back the mindlessness of our early encounters. She'd bounce furiously on top of me, roll off, and fall into a sound sleep. When she awakened she started all over again, if I was still there. But it was not only her indifference to my emotions that was the problem; there were times when she was downright destructive towards me. While from a rational point of view she knew it was best that I didn't drink, she found the thought of my staggering in the front door to be such a turn-on that she often pressured me to go out and get wasted. I'd already had a few close calls, prompted by the promise of even more hellishly passionate sex, and I began to wonder about her. What was it the two of us really shared? What defined our relationship? How could I feel Monica cared about me when she encouraged me to do destructive things to satisfy her own sexual appetite?

"Can I make a suggestion?" General Shapiro said during a session when Monica described the thrill she had felt blowing me in front of Duchamp's *Nude Descending Staircase*, even though it was neither an abstract expressionist work nor an original (it was a reproduction we had spotted in the window of the framing store in town). Monica was talking about the incident as if it were progress. She was hoping to go backwards in art history as a way of combating her addiction. If she could end up getting turned on by an Ingres or even by one of the French academicians, she would be making headway. Pleasure wouldn't be so dependent on fetishes; consequently, I would no longer have to remind her of an alcoholic (either in a sober or inebriated condition) to be attractive to her again. In fact, once the obsession was removed from her, she would undoubtedly go back to her earlier state when the smell of alcohol on my breath was a sickening reminder of her father.

"I have a homework assignment for you."

Monica wasn't going to give Shapiro the pleasure of asking *what?*

"Abstain from sex."

"What about him?"

"His homework is to lay off the bottle."

"A day at a time," I piped in, though General Shapiro didn't hear me since he immediately asked Monica, "May I make a point?"

When she characteristically didn't give him the respect of answering, he asked again, "May I?"

"Does it matter whether I say yes or no? You're going to make your point anyway."

"I want to hear his point," I interjected. "What's your point?"

"It's really striking how every time I try to help you folks, Monica always tries to stop me."

"This doesn't help me." Monica crossed her arms defiantly.

"I don't think you want to be happy," Shapiro insisted. "It makes you anxious. Then people will be jealous of you."

"Was that your point?" I asked.

"No." Shapiro plainly wasn't interested in what I had to say.

"What was it?" I persisted.

"Monica doesn't want to hear it; it makes her too anxious."

"Would you reassure him that it won't make you too anxious so we can get on with the session," I pleaded. "I mean, we're making more out of this... no point is so earthshaking...."

"That's precisely my point," Shapiro interrupted.

"That was your point?"

"No, that wasn't the point," he said. "It's another point."

"Why did you say 'precisely my point' if it wasn't the point?" I said. "It's confusing."

"It's just an expression."

"Maybe you could find some other way of introducing your so-called point that was more palatable to Monica. You might for instance not keep insisting on making your point. Just say what you have to say, and she won't feel you're trying to shove something down her throat. She won't feel you're trying to win."

"I don't mind if he tries to shove something down my throat as long as it's your cock."

That was one session that ended without General Shapiro being able to make his point, and it made me think that somewhere inside of her, Monica had the genes of a segregationist Southern senator circa 1964, filibustering against civil rights legislation.

But something had to crack. We were struggling. Monica and I had never been in each other's company without fucking our brains out. Living together was another matter entirely. We didn't know how to do basic things like stand, talk, read the paper in an armchair, watch television—without having our orifices filled—and despite Monica's seeming resistance, the enjoyment of the more mundane pleasures of romance was something she secretly longed for. Following Shapiro's advice and attempting total abstention turned our lives upside down.

❦

Monica is an ethical person at heart. So whenever we got a call from one of those companies that does surveys, marketing research, and especially opinion polls, she felt it was her civic duty to respond. In the past, the only problem was that she was usually too horny to make it through a telephone conversation. About halfway into the interview, she'd motion to me. I'd walk over and she'd unzip my fly. Then she would take my cock in her mouth, sucking on it with a self-satisfied grin, and only taking it out when she had to clarify a point. Because her mouth was stuffed, she'd often have to repeat her answers, but she was inevitably gracious and cooperative. Monica was always willing to lend a hand if she had a prick in the other. Now, however, it was getting to the point where she was having no trouble answering the questions, since she had nothing in her mouth.

We sat in an embarrassed silence, not knowing what to do with each other now that the magic of our sexual electricity was gone. Extending the electrical metaphor, I'd say the plug was still working all right, but the socket was dead. I had no problems sticking it in whenever she wanted, but she was as dry as the most dried-out patch of the Sahara Dessert on a 120-degree day.

❦

"I'm no expert on art, but it's my impression the abstract expressionists were very contentious. They liked to talk and converse at this place called the Cedar Tavern. There were tremendous fights that sometimes got physical. Drinking wasn't the only thing they did." Usually General Shapiro would wait for one of us to say something. Then he would interrupt before we finished a sentence. That was the essence of his method.

Everyone has their story. The story is what makes people feel special, and it's this uniqueness that General Shapiro chopped down the minute you walked into his office. But today was different; he didn't even wait for us to bother to report what was going on in the relationship since the last time he'd seen us. He was past that. He no longer needed our input at all. He knew. I have to admit he was right, but there still seemed to be something unscientific about reaching conclusions without the benefit of data or observations.

"What if James just fights with you about art instead of being an abusive drunk? Now, James, whatever you do, don't agree with her. You have to swagger to be a good abstract expressionist, and you have to be a sexist. Constantly attack the validity of a woman having opinions. Come on to her when she is trying to talk. Treat her as dismissively as possible and she'll want you just as much as she did when you drunkenly stumbled in the front door of your bunker."

Because Monica and I had never conversed in a normal way, full-fledged arguments about the nature of art were quite a mountain to climb. During the cab ride home, we decided we had to give it a try, but neither of us knew what to do.

"Do we just start talking?" I asked when we walked into the bunker.

Monica shrugged. She knew how to be contentious, but not being a true intellectual, she didn't have an arsenal of provocative remarks to start us off.

"I guess you should say something that gets my goat about art or painting or abstract expressionism," I offered.

The problem was, Monica never had any opinions about abstract expressionism; paint being slapped all over the canvas in the exuberant way it was in the work of Pollock, DeKooning, Motherwell, and Rothko just turned her on. Monica had to feel something about art other than it did or didn't make her horny. She had to come up with an idea about it, and I had to find the idea puerile and annoying. Then I had to berate her and somehow relate her simplistic ideas about art to her family background and upbringing. Once the criticizing began, I would try to fuck her.

"Okay listen, here's an idea: just say 'Franz Kline was influenced by Velasquez.'"

"Franz Kline was influenced by Velasquez."

"That's really dumb. What does a dumb bitch like you know about anything? What'd you read that in *Time* magazine? Are you going to throw that reductive bullshit out at the next lawn party. It's bourgeois. Now get down on all fours, bitch, and I'll put it up your ass."

Monica looked like she was going to swoon. Her face grew red, and she immediately pulled her jeans down to her ankles and got on the floor.

"Oh yeah, put it up my ass. I'm so hot, fuck me, fuck me, fuck me up the ass."

"Say 'Pollock is synchronistic.'"

"Pollock is synchronistic."

"That's what everyone who doesn't understand the narrative element in Pollock says. Synchronistic! What do you know about painting? Now just shut up and suck my cock."

Even though my cock had been in her asshole, she turned around and greedily took it in her mouth. She wanted me. She wanted me as much as she ever had before. It reminded me of the lights going on after a blackout. The increased verbal communication had created a powerful physical attraction. I only hoped that Monica would finally show her gratitude by acknowledging to General Shapiro that he'd been of help.

⚘

"I have a question." General Shapiro and I looked at each other wide-eyed with amazement. We had just walked into the office the morning after a night in which Monica had expressed one harebrained idea about art after the other. I had responded with a series of sexual assaults that she welcomed. During one incident, after she told me that some abstract expressionism reminded her of the markings on the famous Lascaux caves, I rode her like a horse, slapping her behind and yelling, "Heah, heah giddy up!"

"Maybe you can be of help. Does this new thing we're doing mean that every time I express myself, I'm going to get a cock stuck in my mouth, cunt, or ass?"

"What's striking to me is that you have a very high standard. You can never be satisfied or happy. Before, the only thing that turned you on was museums. Now, you're having typically one-sided conversations with a bullying artist intellectual who treats you like a prostitute every time you open your mouth, demeans you, and obliterates any vestige of self-confidence you might be trying to develop about your ability to have opinions. This is progress. There are limits. Your perfectionism, your inability to appreciate your own limits, was making it impossible for you to be happy. The question is, can you be satisfied with this compromise, however imperfect it might be?"

I was distracted. I remembered an item on the E! channel about a new bit that some S&M couples had purchased for each other on Valentine's Day. When you wanted to ride your wife, you just stuck it in her mouth and grabbed the reins. It would be a convenient way to deal with Monica's growing interests in art and politics.

I didn't mind screaming at Monica and berating her; it was better than getting drunk, but I was feeling a resentment, which

I expressed in AA, about the fact that I had to keep supplying her with stupid things to say. I was constantly running out to the magazine stores, searching out opinions in the kind of trendy magazines with the facile overviews that were such an effective lubricant for us. Fashion publications are notorious for presenting a superficial view of the art world. So if there was a De Kooning retrospective at MOMA, I'd run to get the *Vogue* review, which I'd leave next to Monica's side of the waterbed. By the next day, I'd be pulling her hair, screaming at her for being a "decadent bourgeois" while Greek-fucking her in the middle of the kitchen. Naturally, Ting would be waiting outside the window with our order, frantically pulling at himself as he watched me thrusting into her and moving her across the floor.

Robert Hughes, the Australian art critic who specializes in modernism, eventually became a great help to our sex life. In fact, he was not only a help, but a virtual sex aid, a walking Masters and Johnson, a human form of Viagra. I purchased a volume of Hughes' essays after Shapiro had whispered, "Robert Hughes," into my ear as we were leaving one session. Having left the volume on Monica's pillow, I came in one afternoon to find her lying in bed spread eagled with two fingers in her cunt and an essay on the legacy of abstract expressionism in her free hand. She was moaning loudly. I took my clothes off thinking she would want a good fuck. She quickly covered herself up.

"I'm really excited about this." She held up the book. "I'm just loving it, just reading the names. The way he goes into the lives of the painters and lets you see what d'ya call it, lets yuh see about all the painters that came before."

"You mean he gives you the historical context for the rise of abstract expressionism."

"Yeah, how did you know?" she asked, playing dumb so she could indulge her desire to be cut down.

"You're a dumb bitch and a cunt. Just remember that. You

don't have a brain in your head. All you're good for is a good hard fucking." Like magic, my words caused her to throw the sheet off. She spread her legs and started playing with herself again, only this time it wasn't a prelude to talk.

"Come over heah and give me a taste of your big hard cock, sailor." As I lowered myself onto her and shoved my dick into her hot pussy, she let out a cry whose resonance I hadn't heard since Stratford, Ontario, where the actress playing Jocasta in a production of Sophocles' *Oedipus Rex* had let out an animal utterance that sent a shiver down my spine. The only difference with Monica was that hers was a cry of joy, though its shrillness made it seem like anguish.

In the meanwhile, even though I had stopped drinking after my first day of inebriation, and even though my qualification, as they say in the program, only concerned one day, I was a loyal participant in meetings. *You don't have to take the elevator to the bottom* is a famous AA saying, along with *one day at a time*—an expression that had particular meaning for me due to the duration of my drinking career. Scarcely a day went by when I didn't go to a meeting, and soon I found myself elected chairman of the meeting in the very church basement where I'd attended my first day in AA. Isn't it amazing how life comes full circle? They say there are no coincidences. Everything is part of God's plan, and here I was at the break between the qualification and the sharing from the floor, sanctimoniously intoning, "Anonymity is a spiritual part of our program, ever reminding us to place principles over personalities. In other words, what you see here and hear here, leave it here." I was as compulsive in attending my meetings as Monica was in coming out with derivative critiques of abstract expressionism so I could berate her into a state of sexual ecstasy.

But we were running into yet another problem. AA is a program of honesty. Wasn't I harming Monica to criticize her so cruelly? Was it wrong of me to do something harmful to her, even if that harmful thing brought about pleasure? And should I have promptly admitted I was wrong even though it would have eliminated Monica's desire for me?

I dealt with all these problems in the meetings. Another AA slogan is *progress, not perfection*. I felt bad about berating Monica, pulling her by the hair, and even punching her, as I did on one occasion when she said that Larry Rivers reminded her of Rembrandt; but if she enjoyed it, who was I to adjudicate another person's pleasures? Life was a mystery. They say *seek and ye shall find*.

Since Monica was in a relationship with an alcoholic, she qualified for Al Anon, but when I mentioned the Al Anon slogan *detach with love*, she became apoplectic. For someone who thought nothing about throwing her legs around my waist in an attempt at midair copulation, the notion of detachment was a hard concept to grasp. Monica was also not interested in some of the other ideas that came up in recovery meetings, like *sitting with your feelings*. The only way she was going to sit was on my lap with a cock between her legs—a position that contradicted some of the basic premises of the Al Anon program.

I was more dependent on General Shapiro than ever. At times, I felt like a lucky man. I was living the American dream, getting my brains fucked out night and day with no strings attached; Monica was too busy being horny to think about marriage or babies. What she dreamt about was what she had— the equivalent of a brutal abstract expressionist who subjugated her to his ideas and pushed her around before throwing her down on the bed. At other times I felt I was living a nightmare of brutality in which I was controlling another human being for my own invidious purposes. Only General Shapiro could effectively wean Monica from her outdated ideas. Part of the therapy was to build up her self-confidence. Shapiro was walking a fine line. How could he get rid of the sex kitten without losing the sex?

ㅤㅤㅤㅤㅤㅤㅤㅤ**ೞ**

It was after a particularly productive session, during which Shapiro had been working with Monica on being more assertive (his technique was to provoke her so as to get her to argue with him), that I came home to find Monica rolling naked on a sheet of plastic that was covered with a mixture of paints. When she saw me she stared up longingly, spread her legs, and started to play with herself. Even I knew that body painting and action painting had nothing in common, but this time I kept my mouth shut. She was already turned on. She didn't need me. My reluctance to demean her was an act of love. But what resulted was a far cry from our usual passion. We made love, but the feeling of oneness was gone.

It remained to be seen whether the mixture of masturbation and self-assertion could bring about the hot sex we'd had when I was pulling her by the hair, pinching her, and slapping her around. And I didn't have to wait long to find out. General Shapiro had ignited something I had never seen in Monica before. In the past, when we went into a session, Monica would fold her arms around her chest and wait for Shapiro to make a statement, which she would then pull apart. She had spent a good portion of the couples counseling trying to attack his credibility. Now it was apparent that General Shapiro had something she wanted. She went after his ideas as greedily as she grabbed my dick when she was horny. Her lust for knowledge was becoming as great if not greater than her lust for sex. She was opening her mind with the same abandon with which she'd spread her legs.

"You're an intelligent woman," General Shapiro said at one point. Still acting the dumb broad, Monica looked around to see if someone else was in the room. Shapiro caught it. I crossed my fingers, hoping he wasn't going to remark on it. Monica still had her defensiveness. When Shapiro said something about her, she took it as a criticism, even when he meant to be helpful. Of course, Shapiro couldn't resist being right.

"Who are you looking for?" he barked. "See, that's my point. It's striking how you have no belief in your own abilities." Naturally Monica grew silent, but she was learning instead of fighting back. The next day when I came home from my AA meeting, I found her sitting naked in the upholstered armchair that sat in front of the TV. She'd pulled her legs up against her chest. She had a vibrator in one hand, a paint brush in another, and a pad between her legs. She was making figures that almost looked like Chinese ideograms. She'd make a stroke with her right hand, while pressing the vibrator against her pussy with her left. She moaned softly to herself as she came, but the moaning lacked the desperation that had formerly accompanied her orgasms. It was almost like singing. After she was done, she got dressed and asked me if I wanted to go out for dinner. We hadn't gone to a restaurant since our first two dates at The Golden Cock.

I was taken aback at first. *Dinner? Go out?* The words had become foreign. I wasn't sure how to process them. Dinner usually meant ordering in Chinese and seeing Ting's face up against the window of the bunker as I straddled Monica's writhing body. I would be lying if I said I didn't feel a sense of loss, but I wasn't angry or frustrated. I was no more interested in getting into her pants than she was in mine, though I wasn't necessarily happy about the new state of affairs either. I was scared. What would it mean for our relationship? I needed my friends from the AA group or General Shapiro, but it would be hours before my next meeting and days before our next appointment.

"You wanna go back to The Golden Cock? I actually liked the food."

I myself felt ambivalent about The Golden Cock, but my anxiety and apprehension had made me go blank. Besides The Golden Cock, the only other restaurant that came to mind was Domino's Pizza. I said, "That's too fussy."

"You want a steak?" She frowned.

"Too greasy."

"How about Japanese?"

"I don't feel like raw fish."

As we were discussing where to go for dinner, arguing and not being able to agree on something that could never be as enjoyable as our moments of ecstatic sexuality, I realized *this is what it's like to have a mature relationship. This is what General Shapiro has been talking about.*

We decided on Frank's, a cute little place on Chapel Street, around the corner from the bus station. There were cheery waitresses with little white aprons on their gray uniforms, a maitre d' with a blue blazer, and a bathroom with one urinal and one stall, expressly designed to eliminate the possibility of extracurricular activities. There was barely room enough for an adult's knees between the toilet bowl and the stall door. I thought back fondly to the bathroom of The Golden Cock, which was larger and more spacious than the main dining room. When I'd first looked in through the large window, with *Frank's* painted on it in elegant script, I'd seen gray-haired men and women who seemed in many cases to be more intent on studying either the menu or the food on their plates than in paying attention to each other. Frank's provided its customers a mixture of comfort and subdued isolation. The candlelight on each table was less a prelude to romance than a memento to something that'd passed, like the candles you light in a church in memory of the dead. We were never going to fit in with this staid older crowd, but the first thing that Monica said when we were seated was, "Isn't this nice? It's pleasant, eh?" There was one tense moment when she was drawing on a pad and actually got turned on enough to stick her hand in her pants, but we'd finished dessert and were getting ready to leave anyway.

As we walked out of the restaurant, a portly matron with a cane, whose face was covered by a big red hat, ambled passed us.

"Cocksucker, I've been looking for you." I would have recognized the high-pitched voice of Heather Tnapsack anywhere. I didn't know how she'd found me, and I didn't want to know.

"Let's get out of here." I pulled Monica by the arm just as Heather started to come after me with her cane, quivering, "Fuck me already, you son-of-a-bitch; I can't stand it." Monica didn't even ask what the commotion was all about. Sex-crazed old ladies were just the latest consequence of El Niño.

❧

In the past, we started fucking before Ting came with the food and we were all over each other before I had finished my chow mein. By the second fuck of the evening, Ting would have already shot his load all over the window. We were no longer able to see him or he us and there were times when Monica was so turned on that she would stick the egg roll in her cunt, and I would end up finishing dinner between her legs. But recently, since we had been seeing General Shapiro again and were trying to build a real relationship, we had started watching television after dinner—something we never had time for before—and instead of fucking before dinner, we talked. Sometimes we talked about theories of art, and my homework was to avoid criticizing her, slapping her around, or pulling her hair, even if it did turn her on. I was no longer a sit-in for Pollock or DeKooning. I was just James Moran.

After we got home from Frank's, Monica flipped on the tube and we sat on the sofa and watched. One of our problems was that as we became ourselves—which happened more every day—we began to have different interests. I liked "Sixty Minutes," and Monica, "Survivor." She gravitated to reality television while I sought out the old news-magazine format. When we had just been a hot cock and wet cunt, our tastes hadn't mattered, but now we were two separate people and I had to deal with the fact that Monica could be a pain in the ass when she didn't get to see the programs she wanted.

The couples counseling seemed to be winding down, not because Monica and I wanted it to stop, but because General Shapiro had begun to schedule other patients for our hours. We were both confused by this behavior, though this had been his way from the start. One day he would refuse to see you unless you were coming three times a week, and a month later he would simply refuse to see you. Try as we might, we failed to come up with any explanations for these changes. We'd assumed that patients would discuss these matters with a therapist, but then again, Shapiro was a military man. During one of the last sessions, I candidly talked about my complaints and fears. When it came to his own erratic behavior, General Shapiro was uncooperative—as I knew he would be—but when I brought up the matter of our declining interest in sex, he was more forthcoming.

"Yes, you're not as sexual. You're experiencing your limits. You can't have everything. If you want to become real people you have to experience boundaries. That's reality, James. Before, you were living in a state of polymorphous perversity, but you didn't have any selves. Now you have well-defined personalities. You have likes and dislikes. You argue over what foods you like and what to watch on the tube. That's what marriage is for most people. That's love. From my perspective, you folks love each other very much."

Shapiro crossed his arms after gently running his fingers through his phantom hair. We had a half an hour to go in our session, but he looked like a man who didn't need to say another word. I kept thinking about the hunting metaphor and the stuffed heads on the walls. If he was going to be truthful, he'd have to be our taxidermist rather than our couples counselor; then he'd have true renderings of the creatures he'd subdued. There was no doubt he was satisfied with his work.

We'd always driven or called for a taxi to take us back and forth from Shapiro's office, but since Monica was no longer compelled to run home to roll in paint and play Eliza Doolittle to my latter-day Henry Higgins, Helen Frankenthaler to my bullying Clement Greenberg in abstractionist terms, we had started to walk. Our town is full of little bits of late Victoriana—many of the old mansions have turrets—that were fun to study and talk about on the way home. But after that penultimate session, Monica insisted we call a cab, and once we were in the cab, she was sullen and unforthcoming.

"I thought you would want to celebrate."

"You don't get it, do you? He wants to give our hour away to someone else."

"We pay our bills."

"He realizes we're on the way out and he spotted some new prey on the horizon. If he doesn't snare them quickly...."

"Hold on a second. General Shapiro made it very clear he wanted to help us."

"He wanted to help us, and now that he's helped us, he wants to get rid of us. Love indeed!"

"You don't think we love each other?"

"Well, what's your opinion, James?"

"I asked you."

"I don't call it love when you refuse to even watch one episode of 'Survivor' with me."

"Lots of couples watch different television programs."

"Okay, fine. Let's buy two TVs. You go in the bedroom, and I'll watch in the living room." Our changing interests clearly dictated new design options. The bedroom would be decorated with a "Sixty Minutes" news magazine décor while the living room would be the more lived-in reality-television environment.

❧

Our last session with General Shapiro was devoted almost entirely to our problems watching television. Monica wanted me to be something I wasn't—a lover of reality television. Again the problem of limits was coming up. Monica's inability to accept the imperfection of the universe was causing her unhappiness. But General Shapiro was distracted, even bored. He kept looking at his door, as if anticipating some new arrival—some inchoate bit of matter, the unformed clay of the maladaptive relationship that he could mold into a new trophy, a new testament to his talents as a healer.

Monica grudgingly began to accept that Sunday night was a special time for me. I'd come to cherish "Sixty Minutes," which is the grandfather of all the great television-magazine programs. She came to understand I would be a little more distracted, a little less attentive to her interests because I had just watched "Sixty Minutes." We were both learning to accommodate our likes and dislikes. After "Sixty Minutes" was over, I generally experienced some degree of depression and she left me alone. There had been some rough Sundays when she watched something after "Sixty Minutes" and sought validation for her feelings of excitement about the program. But she came to understand she didn't need me to affirm her. She'd made a choice and that was enough. Constantly asking me, "What do you think, isn't such and such exciting, romantic, suspenseful?"—when I was depressed about having to wait another week until the next "Sixty Minutes"—had caused several spats. We were growing. And there were moments when Monica paused from her own excitement to exhibit sympathy for the loss I was feeling. That was also progress.

We both realized there was no need for the bunker. When we'd first found the concrete cinderblock structure in the deserted factory area of town, it felt like an oasis. We were able to fuck without causing structural damage to the edifice we occupied. It was probably the way people prone to grand mal seizures feel after waking up to find themselves in a safe, padded cell. But with our life changing, we had new requirements when it came to real estate, one of which was our enduring interest in ordering in Chinese food. Now that we weren't fucking our brains out, Ting looked bored, and we were back to square one when it came to calling for deliveries. It took hours for him to come, and he'd often send replacements who couldn't find our address. When they did, they could be surly, uncooperative, and perpetually argumentative about the tip. We needed to move to a place that was closer to the major Chinese restaurants so we could get our food delivered in a timely manner. On Sundays, with everyone in town ordering in Chinese food, we were never going to get what we wanted in time to watch our programs. Of course we could order hours in advance to insure we'd get it in time for say, "Sixty Minutes," but then the food would be traveling around on some delivery boy's bicycle and it would arrive cold.

I was also getting tired. It's hard enough trying to communicate with the Chinese people taking the orders; every time I gave my address, there would be a long silence. In the background, I'd hear urgent voices talking the Mandarin dialect. I don't know too many Chinese restaurants that turn down customers. So they'd reluctantly take the order, but there was much irritation, especially when we tried to confirm the number of rices that came with the main dishes or we asked for an extra bag of noodles with the wonton soup.

We had been fucking our brains out at the time we rented the bunker, so naturally neither of us remembered signing any leases but apparently we had. We made an appointment with our landlord, John, who turned out to be a recovering sex addict himself. When we explained to him that when we had moved in six months before, we had been young and inexperienced, but were now trying to build decent lives in which we could watch television together, he was fully understanding of our plight. He admitted he was aware we were going to be a handful from the moment his property manager described the shenanigans that went on in the rental office. On the other hand he knew the concrete bunker was the safest structure in town when it came to turbulence within the psyche or without. The bunker had also had a sobering effect on the previous tenants, a couple so enamored of each other that paramedics had to be called on several occasions to pry them apart. He said he was glad that letting ourselves play out our tumultuous love, without the interruption of neighbors complaining about broken beams or chipping plaster, had brought us back to our senses. He happily cancelled our lease. We had a week to move out and find a new place. During that week, several real estate brokers came by with prospective tenants—including a pair of lesbians who were leaders of our town's only female motorcycle gang, a dominatrix who wanted to turn the place into a dungeon, and a married couple who hated each other, but couldn't imagine what life would be like without their constant fighting.

We left our waterbed. We told each other it was leaking and about to burst, but neither of us wanted to admit we no longer needed it. Waterbeds are great when you spend most of your time fucking, but they're terrible when you're tired and need to simply fall asleep. They never stop undulating and you can actually get motion sickness if you're the type of person who needs to read before sleeping. We were lucky we were able to get our old apartment back. In addition, Bill was looking for an excuse to break away from his aerobics teacher, who'd become too possessive. He was happy to cook us a welcome-home dinner. Bill was still in love with me, but he was no longer jealous of my relationship with Monica, and that first night back we all noted how well we got along.

Bill liked reality programs like "Survivor," as well as news magazines like "Sixty Minutes," and as time went on he became more and more of a presence in the house. In the past, when we were fucking all the time, we would never have been able to have dinner guests and we didn't need them. But now that we were more well adjusted—and not driven to ripping each other's clothes off whenever we could—I for one felt a certain hole in our lives, a hole that had formerly been occupied by sex and now would be filled with socializing.

Then there was Bill's cooking. While I still loved Chinese, Monica, in particular, started craving more variety, and Bill was a virtual lexicon of specialties, from his meatloaf to more exotic fare like grilled squid, corn fritters, and conch. We were both unselfconsciously gaining weight and loving it.

As we grew closer to Bill, our eating and television-watching took on an intensity and variety that rivaled our most passionate sexual episodes. Every meal had a significance, both in terms of the ingredients and amounts we were consuming and in terms of the television programs we watched. Bill showed up early for "The Today Show" and cooked everything from porridge to kippers and pancakes. Lunch celebrated the beginning of the afternoon soaps and was thus one of our most important meals. Fish chowder and bouillabaisse appetizers were followed by Bill's famous caesar salad and then a hearty dish like osso buco.

Bill was opposed to the stereotypic notion that lunch should be a light, practical meal composed only of pasta and salad. Lunch was an issue for Bill. He felt it was slighted, the very way he had felt slighted and marginalized as a homosexual male. Now that sex was no longer the *lingua franca* of the household, the playing field was more leveled, but Bill's lunches were almost like crusades. There was an ideological consistency to his insistence that they last from two to three hours, just in time for the three of us to take our warm alcohol-free zabagliones into the living room to watch "Oprah." The large lunches didn't stop Bill from preparing high tea or even larger and more elaborate dinners, and on weekends and holidays, Bill even cooked up a midnight buffet. Within weeks, our apartment was like a cruise ship—at least from the culinary point of view.

Bill could be as temperamental as an artist, and in many ways his fits, in which he would throw a perfectly good paella, coq au vin, or leg of lamb into the garbage, reminded me of the creative agonies of Pollock and DeKooning. I could see that Monica received some degree of stimulation from the scenes Bill threw, and it was a good thing he was gay or she might have had a full-fledged regression. Luckily there had been no gay abstract expressionists, so it was hard for Monica to transfer the powerful emotions she still had for Pollock and DeKooning onto Bill. Larry Rivers was AC/DC, yet he was a pop artist, and Monica had never been stimulated by the work of Andy Warhol, Rauschenberg, or Johns. If she had been, then there would have been no problem in her wanting to fuck a gay man. The *hypergraphia satyriasis* would have kicked in, and we would have been off to the races. As it was, Monica, Bill, and I looked forward to shopping at Sam's Club, the warehouse food outlet off the interstate where you could buy 1000-roll packages of toilet paper, ten-gallon drums of orange juice, and boxes that contained 12 dozen eggs. We went there on Tuesdays and

Fridays after dinner, which gave us something to do related to food when we were inundated with feelings of loss over a meal ending. We might have been stuffed, considering the enormous amounts Bill cooked, but all the lust we had for each other was now shifted to varying dishes, and the end of our meals inevitably left us feeling restless, bored, and yearning for the kind of excitement only a discount food outlet could provide.

Besides the arguments about reality television versus news magazines, which had been subsiding, the three of us got into arguments about what to eat for dinner or, on occasions when we went out, what restaurant to go to, reminding me of the kind of relationships where couples argue about how and when to have sex. When it came to sex, there had never been a struggle since our sex transcended consciousness. When it came to our appetites for food, we were afflicted with too much consciousness. Monica and I became competitive and somewhat anal-retentive, and Bill, who placed such store on his refined taste, didn't make things any better. As far as I was concerned (and in spite of the increased sensitivity of my palate) I could have ordered in Chinese food until the cows came home, but Monica, who complained about my lack of adventurousness (another comment common to couples who argue about sex), was aligning herself with Bill, who was becoming a snob. Despite his humble origins, he began to display the characteristics of a landed aristocrat. He'd developed a peculiar sneer that was half Oxford don and half rearing horse. The stability of our little ménage was beginning to be threatened by the alliance between Monica and Bill against my constant, "I have a craving for Chinese," or "It's too much trouble to cook, let's just order in Chinese," or "It's actually cheaper to order in the Chinese than to go out and buy the ingredients for a meal."

One thing I learned in my AA meetings was acceptance. We are all children of God and everything is as it's meant to be, though I have to say that when I go two or three days without ordering in Chinese, I start to get irritable. And if I'm going to watch "Sixty Minutes" or any of the other magazine shows, Chinese is a requirement. I'm basically an easygoing guy, but I'd say that in general if I'm deprived of my Chinese on Sunday, I can get depressed and even aggressive. On one occasion when I was deprived of both "Sixty Minutes" and Chinese, my Tourette's was ignited and I started yelling, "Fuck you, mommy." I would have been the first to admit I was a Chinese food addict, but there are worse things one can be addicted to. Destructive sex that ruins other people's apartments is one example. My obsession with Chinese food wasn't hurting anyone, and from a health standpoint I had been switching from sautéed broccoli in garlic sauce to steamed broccoli in oyster sauce, from white rice to brown rice, from chow fun to steamed vermicelli noodles. Sure, repetition can be confining, but as Emily Dickenson once said about her resistance to change, "I know Amherst well."

"I don't call fortune cookies *almond cookies* or those little pieces of pineapple and orange sections they give you in Chinese restaurants *dessert*." Bill's tone was sardonic, but I knew he was hurting. Our differences were creating an even greater rift than had occurred when I refused to let him suck my cock.

There were times when I thought the three of us should see General Shapiro, who had told us when we left that he would always find time for us if we ever wanted to come back, while at the same time making it absolutely clear that he didn't have any time left in his schedule. This was just one of the paradoxes of the treatment. Another was the fact that he could talk endlessly about himself and his marriage heroics on the couples counseling battlefield, but when you asked him about his personal life, he would admonishingly say, "I thought we were here to talk about you." I wanted to talk to him about food and sex and ask him how he decided what to eat and where to go to dinner with his wife, but I knew he was going to give me that quizzical stare that turned wishes into neuroses. Yes, there was something wrong with me, and one of the chief symptoms was that I wanted him to tell me what to do. Yes, I knew it wouldn't do any good. I was going to have to work the food thing out with Monica and Bill on my own.

I was willing to negotiate the reality television. I was equally willing to try new foods and even eat out now and then. Yet the cornerstone of any negotiation had to be take-out Chinese and "Sixty Minutes" on Sunday nights. Beyond that, I was open to suggestions, provided there was at least one other day of the week that we all agreed to order in Chinese. We could have Rumanian cuisine for all I cared, as long as it wasn't on Sunday and as long as it left room for one other day when I could have the wonton soup, egg roll, and chicken chow mein, the combination plate referred to in shorthand by cognoscenti around the world as *the number one.*

We finally agreed on Sunday and Thursday. I still loved Bill's meatloaf, but he was hell-bent on creativity. He didn't like having the same comfortable foods all the time. He said experiment was at the heart of truly great cuisine. He wanted to try new things, to experience tastes and sensations he hadn't tried before. What he said he liked was an implicit criticism of me. I am a creature of habit and the same old things are what make me happy. A new taste or smell is like a strange city or foreign country. It's okay to be a tourist now and then. However, I like to get home. What I like when it comes to food is what I know; it's rare that I'm able to assimilate a new taste or texture. But I gave in, feeling like a rat in a laboratory experiment and gritting my teeth through a hundred meals that were memorable in the displeasure they caused. I don't differentiate one Chinese meal from the other and I don't remember any of them, but that's what I like.

I actually felt that part of Bill's and Monica's pleasure in sampling the cuisines of the world came from seeing me suffer. And God forbid if it turned out I liked a dish. That was a sure guarantee I'd never taste it again. Look what happened when Bill made hummus: He showed me how you smear the "homos" on a wedge of pita bread, add cucumber, tomato, and a touch of mint, and I loved it. The next day, I was jumping for joy. Finally, he'd come up with a new dish that was not only edible, but delicious. I immediately said, "Let's have 'homos' again soon. I love 'homos.'"

"What you mean to say is that some of your best friends are homos."

"It's hummus!" Monica admonished.

"Homos." I repeated.

"No, hummus. The accent is on the first syllable, and you have to make a little *chhhhh* sound with roof of your mouth. *Chhhommos!* Say it."

"Chhhummus."

Needless to say, even though I finally got the pronunciation of hummus, I wasn't offered any after that night, although I did get to try some very enticing dishes, amongst them duck with prune stuffing, lamb shank with olives and lemon, and choucroute. I wish I could say Monica was one of those dishes. Back when I couldn't find Monica, I went through my period of being overweight, but at least I was aware of it. I was afraid I would be unrecognizable, that no one would know me under the layers of fat; but when Monica lost her boyish figure, she didn't seem to care.

After all we'd been through, I'd become attached to her; I wasn't going to leave her. However, I often wondered if her mind wasn't drowning in all the flesh she was putting on. It used to be that our waterbed was in danger of busting. Now that we had a regular bed, the problem was Monica's heaviness, which created a trough at the center. It was particularly difficult to read a magazine before I went to sleep because every time Monica shifted, I would roll into her—something that wasn't helped by the fact that I was beginning to have a weight problem of my own. I wanted to say something, yet I didn't know what I could say without risking eliciting her animal rage. She loved her meals so much. I also didn't want to do anything to inhibit the healthy interest in food that was the fruit of all our work with General Shapiro.

Gradually, I found myself getting caught up in the food hysteria. Along with my two Chinese meals, I began to look forward to my Bries and Camemberts, my terrines and fois gras. I loved "Sixty Minutes II" almost as much as "Sixty Minutes," but I couldn't resist "The Apprentice," which led me to "Who Wants to Be a Millionaire?" "Survivor," and even "Fear Factor." Soon it didn't matter what I was watching as long as I had something in my mouth, just as it didn't matter what I was eating as long as something was on the tube.

Along the way, Bill and Monica were becoming interested in fine wines. There was constant talk of Chateau this or that, the grand crus and the premier grand crus, and arguments about the excellence of unattainably expensive wines like the Lafitte Rothschild '66. Naturally, because of my ongoing membership in AA, I stayed out of these discussions, but I was satisfied. With my tastes for both food and television expanding almost as quickly as my waist, I was finding a new sense of adventure in life, which I suspect was exactly what General Shapiro was talking about.

Yes, I was fat again, but after all the months of uncertainty and fear, when I'd come to after explosive sex not even knowing where I was, after all the months of haunting art galleries and museums, after all the worrying about landlords and structural damage, I was truly happy and well adjusted for the first time in years. I could just see General Shapiro smiling and, with that false modesty, declaiming, "It's you guys who did the work."

It's not that Monica and I no longer had problems. No couple is immune. General Shapiro used to say, "When you stop having problems, you're either dead or having an affair." But our problems kept changing. Now that sex and food were no longer the issue, we had to contend with our weights and our elevated blood sugars. We lived on the second floor, and it was becoming increasingly hard to walk up the stairs. In addition, Monica's ass had become so big that it sometimes shook the toilet seat from its hinges—but these were designer problems compared to what we had faced in the past. And, in spite of the fact we were no longer having sex, I loved Monica more than ever.

ം

For the longest time I was sure I'd come to the last stop on the line. Monica, Bill, and I never disagreed anymore. Every night exemplified the fact that human beings can live in peace and harmony if they talk out their differences. We'd eat in front of the television together, watching the programs that had been agreed on beforehand. Usually the three of us sat on the couch, pulling over little tray tables, which we stacked in the corner of the kitchen at the end of each meal. There were times when we sat together at the dining table. We did this, for instance, on the night Bill cooked up a fondue and there had to be some place to put the cheese pot. Occasionally we ate at the table when we were having Chinese dishes like Peking duck, which require several different plates (for the sliced duck, the bones, the pancakes, the scallions, and the hoisin sauce). But our dining table was far from the television, and all of us agreed that the distance deprived us of a certain intimacy with whatever program we were watching.

Our bliss seemed complete until the day Bill informed us he

was leaving. There had been no warning, no way of foreseeing he had been unhappy—and he wasn't. He just, as he put it, "wanted something more." Bill was going home to Kansas to live with his mother. Bill's father had been a soybean farmer; as he prospered, he'd employed many farmhands, one of whom had introduced Bill to the pleasures of fellatio. Bill's father had always hated his son's love of cooking and sewing. He was embarrassed by the boy. But his relationship with the farmhand was the last straw. Discovering Bill and the farmhand in an empty silo, he had thrown Bill out of the house despite his mother's protests. Bill's attempt at marriage and fatherhood had been a concession to his father's values. But his failure had sent him into a tailspin; he'd been spared the life of homelessness and self-abnegation by me that day in the bus station. By now his father was long dead, and when he'd written his mother, she'd opened her arms to him. The farm had been sold, and when Bill told his mother of his great dream of running a restaurant that would cater to gay farmhands, called Cock n' Bull, she fully supported the idea. Kansas was no longer the way it had been when he was a boy growing up; there were substantial gay communities, in even the most rural areas, whose needs were waiting to be met.

Monica and I threw Bill a surprise banquet during which we served not only Bill's favorite dishes, but those he had only dreamt of making, like pheasant under glass. That evening the television was his. We placed the remote in a box, wrapped it in beautiful paper, tied a ribbon around it, and handed it to him the minute he walked in. Bill was totally overwhelmed when he walked into the apartment to see the trouble we had gone to, and after all the tears and hugs he insisted I order in Chinese and watch any news magazine I wanted to see—even if they were the lesser ones like "MTV Cribs." He couldn't bear to see me white knuckling it through gourmet dishes and watching reality TV (despite my growing weakness for it) when I was dreaming of Chinese and "Nightline." Even though I was embarrassed, I caved in—especially since my pyorrhea had been acting up again and I needed softer foods like lo mein. I didn't want the evening to end. I had the two people in the world who were most important to me and my most favorite programs and food. Thinking it over afterwards, I realized that Bill hadn't become any more enamored of news magazines or Chinese food; he had just wanted me to be happy during our last moments together. I remarked to myself how curious it was that I didn't feel the same way. I loved Bill and wished him the best. But, after all, we only had one television, and while Bill had been served everything he could have ever desired, he certainly didn't get to see his favorite programs, the way I had been hogging the tube.

The mind can play strange tricks. I had blocked the fact that Bill had departed. I was shocked returning home to an empty kitchen that first night after he left. Now Monica and I were like two siblings left alone to fend for ourselves with the parent gone. I'd been doing some volunteer work for a local amateur theater club which was mounting a revival of *Fiorello*, and when I came home I found Monica lying on the sofa in front of "Oprah" like a beached whale. We'd gotten to the point where we knew each other so well we didn't even need to say anything. Monica went on watching as if I wasn't there.

When "Oprah" ended she said, "I guess we'll just order in some Chinese." I don't know what got into me. I suspect it was some sort of conditioned response provoked by the timing of the finish of the program and the mention of take-out Chinese, but I pulled my dick out of my pants and held it in front of her mouth. She looked at it with the same welcome you might have given a burglar crawling through a bedroom window in the middle of the night. She didn't scream. Her expression was a mixture of amazement, disgust, and fear. I sheepishly stuck my dick back in my pants and flipped our remote to CNN.

Going back to a strict regimen of Chinese food would have perpetuated the same old patterns and would not have been taking into account the growth of Monica's personality—or of her stomach for that matter. I knew that Bill's departure had traumatized her, but Monica also had a tendency to push her feelings down to the deepest recesses of her being, which, considering the increased space her being took up, was now quite a distance from top to bottom. She was plainly sinking into a depression in which nothing mattered. I could have eaten Chinese food everyday and it wouldn't have been a symptom of anything. However, I knew that Monica's willingness to return to our old habits was not a sign of mental health. Monica had been Bill's sous chef and I thought getting her back in the kitchen again would be the answer, though it was important that she start small. I suggested we take time out of our regimented television schedule to hold a marathon screening of recordings of "The Martha Stewart Show" that we'd made when it looked like Martha was headed to prison, but Monica wasn't responsive.

Isn't it odd how help often comes from the most unexpected places? Who would believe a Swanson's Boneless White Meat Fried Chicken Hungry-Man would be the agent of Monica's salvation. But it was a TV dinner that finally cured her of her malaise. We had stopped off to load up on paper towels and toilet paper at Sam's Club when we passed the frozen food section.

"Swanson's TV dinners, I haven't seen one since I was a kid. I didn't think they still made them," Monica cried out with childish glee. Her sexual addiction had started at such a young age that she had bypassed many of the experiences other adolescents have. According to SAA (Sex Addicts Anonymous), emotionally, Monica would be the age she was when she had first started acting out, which in her case was twelve. She had bypassed the junk food stage that most teenagers go through when, by the time she was fourteen, she graduated from hand jobs and heavy petting to affairs with married men who wined her and dined her with fine French cuisine.

She wheeled our cart past the frozen food section, but I ran back and grabbed three Fried Chicken Hungry-Mans and a Roast Turkey. TV dinners are okay as far as I'm concerned, though they don't compare to ordering in Chinese, but we had to start somewhere. A sacrifice was needed if she and I were going to get back on our feet again.

The Hungry-Men led us into a whole new area of microwave cookery. There were frozen pizzas, Kraft Macaroni and Cheese Dinners, frozen fish sticks, turkey pot pies, frozen French fries. Monica became so fat that it would have been difficult to have sex even if we wanted to. I would have needed a pretty big dick to get past her huge hanging stomach and, to be honest, my six inches makes me normal, but not what one would call exceptionally well hung. As our relationship matured, sleeping together took on the literal meaning of the words. I began to enjoy the depression in the bed caused by all her blubber. I'd fall into the trough her body created and warm myself. It was different from putting my dick in her hot hole, yet it was a hole all the same and I came to look forward to it almost as much as I did in the days when *hole* meant something else.

One time in the middle of the night, I had a shock. It was like having a nightmare, only I was awake. I turned to look at her, and due to the darkness and the fat, I barely recognized her face. I was so upset, I actually woke her up. Monica's increased heft required more sleep, and she got very irritated when she was disturbed at night. What a far cry from the days when all I had to do was nudge her with my hard rod and a wet orifice would be waiting for me! But I lied and told her I was having chest pains, then added, "it's probably just gas," so as not to cause too much alarm. I simply had to hear her talk in order to reassure myself that her soul hadn't departed from her body. If it had been daylight, the incident would never have happened. But as Fitzgerald once said, "In a real dark night of the soul it is always three o'clock in the morning." This time it was only 2:45, but that was bad enough.

The days of our fond embraces were over. But a couple learns to find other pleasures. That was General Shapiro's message from the first days of our counseling. And now that Monica was getting interested in microwave cooking, I felt we were hitting our stride. We would sit on the sofa with our tray tables, watching television and eating what in Monica's case turned out to be four or five TV dinners. The Boneless White Meat Fried Chicken Hungry-Man was a favorite we both agreed on, but Monica would go on to a turkey pot pie, a pot roast, a Salisbury steak, mashed potatoes and gravy, and sometimes even the Weight Watchers Fish Sticks, which she gobbled down as the equivalent of an after-dinner *digestif.* My theater work has always come in fits and starts. However, I have my busy periods, which can be disruptive. We were just starting to get used to microwave cooking and TV dinners around the time of the latest episode of "The Apprentice," only to find our idyll broken. I was asked to work on a touring production of *Annie,* which was moving from the Boca Raton Playhouse to Toledo's Center Stage Rep. Monica was going through a vulnerable period and I'd been afraid of leaving, but when I returned we quickly resumed where we had left off, celebrating our first night back together by sampling some of the Banquet line of TV dinners.

While Monica's heft had increased since I first went to bed with her, my stomach had simply become more round. After my first run-in with weight gain, I'd been shaken up. Now with obesity threatening again, I started a program of intensive exercising that became a compulsion in and of itself. Once I saw the benefits of exercise, I couldn't stop. If I was feeling depressed, an hour's worth of exercise would put me in a good mood. If I was planning to eat a bunch of fatty TV dinners, I could either work off the extra calories before I ate or right after. I stopped seeing the point of not exercising. If I was having a talk with Monica, watching TV, or even eating dinner, I'd climb on my stationary bike or grab some hand weights. After all, if I hadn't stayed in shape then I wouldn't have been able to help Monica do basic things like getting up from the sofa. It's always important to have at least one person in a household who isn't suffering from obesity; that way there is someone who can get up quickly and have his wits about him enough to dial 911 if his obese significant other has a stroke or heart attack.

More often than not, Monica was left having dinner alone on the sofa with her tray table while I pedaled on our True, a stationary bike that has a basket in front to hold nuts, fruits, protein bars, and a bottle of water. Trues are enormously stable, but it's still hard to balance a hot meal on the basket top, especially due to the grooves created to hold water bottles. When I wasn't frantically bicycling, I was doing pull-ups or lying on my new bench with its forty-five-pound bar and complementary set of plates. I also kept hand weights, grips, jump ropes, and a Pilates ball nearby. Even though we were only separated by a few feet, we felt miles apart because my interest in getting in shape was causing me to limit my intake of foods, while Monica's *modus operandi* was to intake as much as humanly possible. As I started to see a six-pack emerge from my formerly distended stomach, I wanted to deprive myself, while she increasingly needed more. My improving physical condition, in fact, seemed to egg Monica on. As she watched me pedaling furiously, the beads of sweat accumulating on my forehead, she'd intone, "I know you're going to leave me," while stuffing her mouth with one of the buttered rolls that hung in a plastic bag around her neck in case she needed a snack between meals. She looked a little like a Saint

Bernard with that bag around her neck, but I never complained to her about it.

Despite the fact that we were traveling different roads from the dietary point of view—with me becoming svelte and handsome and her becoming increasingly fat and ugly—Monica and I were building trust. We broached the subject of marriage on several occasions. Usually it's the woman who wants the financial security that marriage provides, but in our case both of us had brought it up at one time or another only to dismiss the necessity of creating a legal bond. We knew that a marriage could be complex and often involved hiring more than one caterer. In our case, there wouldn't have been any question about whom to invite since we had no family or friends besides Bill, and we would hardly have expected Bill to fly in from Kansas. But it would have taken weeks to agree on a menu, and then there would have been the problem of prying Monica away from the buffet to perform a ceremony. Monica had become a responsible adult in many ways, but she could be intransigent when she was hungry. We decided we had enough on our plates as a couple. We didn't need to complicate matters any further by exchanging vows and inviting the government into our lives.

I was still attending my meetings regularly, but in many ways we had become the average American couple. After all, Monica wasn't the only one on our block with obesity problems, and I was no exception when it came to compulsive exercise. You have people who jog and lift weights at all times of the day and night, and you have people in the same family whose hands are in the cookie jar at the same hour.

This polarity was becoming more obvious in our relationship every day. Monica had developed a love for ice cream, which she bought in gallon cartons and ate while watching any program except "Oprah." Considering that Oprah was battling the same weight problems that Monica was facing, it was easy to see why. And I had acquired a new piece of gym equipment that bore a striking resemblance to the rack, the popular medieval torture device. Like a lot of couples, Monica and I perfectly complemented each other. I represented control and she excess. I provided limits and she loosened me up. There was even a "Montel Williams" devoted to this very subject. You displace onto your partner those traits you don't want to deal with yourself.

The one thing we took from General Shapiro was an interest in cultural events and civic affairs. When he told us there were other things in life that a couple could enjoy together besides sex, it was a real eye opener. Now that Monica was no longer losing control of herself in front of abstract expressionist art, she began to see it in a new light. I thought she might end up disenchanted, thinking that abstract expressionism was meaningless scribble and that painters like Pollock had pulled one over on the public, but instead of being disaffected she became interested in the work of Pollock's wife, Lee Krasner, and other female abstractionists like Helen Frankenthaler. Once we had attracted a great deal of attention in museums and restaurants because we couldn't keep our hands off each other; now we were getting sideways glances because of the disparity in our appearances. I was even approached by someone from a group called Fat and Free who wanted to use us as Couple of the Month in their newsletter. And then there were the embarrassing incidents. We never became an object of curiosity the way we were when Monica insisted on having sex in public, but from a practical point of view, Monica didn't fit in certain spaces. For instance, when we tried to eat in a Fifties-style diner that had opened in town, Monica was unable to squeeze into a booth. Rather than feel ashamed, it was at times like this that my heart went out to her and I felt a love and pride in her that I never felt in all our passionate groping. I've always been interested in helping the underdog and I'll support the guy or gal who tries to fulfill his dreams even when the cards are stacked against them—even if the dream is nothing greater than trying to get too much to eat. There was something heroic about Monica trying to prevail in all her obsessions, whether they were sex or art or food.

We did have a last fling, one moment of total debauchery. Like the Proustian Madeleine, it was ignited by the olfactory memory of a thing. In our case, it was a restaurant rather than a pastry. We had been driving home after seeing a production of *The Marriage of Figaro*, which was put on by the local opera society, and we passed The Golden Cock. Monica felt for my prick, which was stiff for the first time in months, and before I knew it she had her face in my crotch. I remembered how talented Monica had been in giving blowjobs, how her mouth seemed to have an almost unlimited capacity for sucking. She was a magician in making large objects disappear into relatively small spaces. But suddenly I noticed a change. Eating has always been the slang for fellatio. As The Golden Cock's neon sign disappeared into my rearview mirror, Monica seemed to be literally eating me. The blowjob was turning into another meal. She licked my cock as if it were a lolly and took my balls into her mouth, running her tongue up and down the sides of my scrotum as if she were wiping gravy off of a plate. If I'd had a piece of baguette on me, I would have offered it to her. Then, as we stopped at a red light and I came, she greedily swallowed my cum as if she were drinking a milk shake.

The moment we got back to the house, the television went on as if nothing had happened. Monica was splayed out on the sofa and I was pedaling furiously on the bike. We'd gotten home just in time for "Sixty Minutes II," which Monica claimed to prefer to "Sixty Minutes." Monica's legs were covered with broken blood vessels and her thighs and ass were thickened with cellulite. She wore dark orthopedic stockings that she rolled up above her knees. Yet I still felt pangs, having tasted the old life (to be precise it was Monica who'd done the actual tasting). Our encounters had been like the seismic shifts of an earthquake that leave a path of open cracks begging to be filled. I wanted her. I jumped off the bike, edged into the little space left on the couch next to her, and threw my arms around her. Monica looked at me as if I were crazy. "You're sweaty" was the only thing she said.

Whenever I'm upset, I've learned to go down for twenty, which in work-out lingo means twenty pushups. In this case, I did twenty pushups, fifty jack knives (because you need to strengthen your central core at times of emotional turmoil), and another twenty pushups on my knuckles with my fists together, which is an excellent way to strengthen the triceps—a muscle that had fallen into disuse since we'd stopped fucking. I wanted to say to Monica *get off the couch, shake it up, do some lunges, do some squats.* I wanted to pass on what I'd learned, but it was too late. Monica had a hard enough time getting up off the couch when she took one of her infrequent breaks from eating and watching television. Even if she could have joined me, I wouldn't have been totally free to enjoy it because of the emissions of gas that came out of her both before and after arising and the horrendous odors that emanated from her when she attempted to move her body. When she got up, she sounded like a car whose distributor cap was broken. There was a little sputtering, like minor sniper fire, followed by an explosion that was remarkably similar to the blast from a twelve-gauge shotgun.

But things had never been perfect, had they? As someone in the program once put it, *there's always a fly in the ointment.* From the day I first laid eyes on Monica—an event which didn't occur until quite a while after we'd begun sexual relations—I didn't remember a time when I hadn't felt something was missing. What I had learnt was that having a relationship requires give and take. Sometimes this giving and taking involved the basics of everyday life. I gave Monica the Swanson's Boneless White Meat Fried Chicken Hungry-Man after I pulled it piping hot from the microwave, and she took it. This giving and taking could involve even simpler activities. In the morning when Monica was finally able to pull herself out of bed after a long night of eating and television-watching, she'd belch, let out couple of loud farts, and then call out from the bathroom, "Where's the toothpaste?" She never remembered where the toothpaste was and I often found myself welling up with anger. I felt put upon. *Why do I have to constantly tell her where the toothpaste is? Why do I have to do everything?* Then a calm came over me when I realized that the joy of a relationship came from being able to give unconditionally. I profited in the act of giving. I was not always able to calculate my reward—especially when I saw Monica glued to the television set with the discarded box from a twelve-pack of Dunkin Donuts sitting by her side—yet, nevertheless, I felt assured it would come. Part of having faith, I'd learned after all the months of recovery, had to do with realizing that though you may not be getting what you want, you are ending up with what you need.

After all the turmoil we had been through, we had finally settled into a routine, but God, if he exists, likes to play tricks. Just at the point when Monica and I achieved the kind of predictable existence that both of us desired—at least in one part of our beings—something came along to upset the apple cart. We were watching television while Monica ate and I rode the stationary bike. We'd been in a state of effortless contentment when Monica swallowed a bone. Whether it's a penis or a piece of food, Monica has always had to have something in her mouth. I had warned her time and time again *eat slowly, chew your food carefully,* but you can't control another person. As they say in the program, *we're powerless over people, places, and things.* And speaking of things, she never listened to a thing I said. In all fairness, the accident might not have occurred if I hadn't mistakenly bought the regular Swanson's Fried Chicken dinner instead of the Boneless White Meat Fried Chicken Hungry-Man which Monica was more accustomed to. I've watched Monica enough to realize she doesn't think when she eats. She probably didn't even notice the difference. A normal person takes note of bones, gristle, and other impediments, but Monica was not likely to pay attention. Her mouth was like a garbage compactor grinding up anything that's put into it—except that unlike a garbage compactor, it was also attached to a human body. A bone was lodged in her trachea and she was gasping for air. I knew both of our lives were on the line. She was the one who looked as if she would die, and I knew I couldn't live without her.

I tried to pick her up so that I could apply the Heimlich maneuver, but she wouldn't budge. She was like a panicked drowning person who becomes a threat to the rescuer. Even as she was gagging, she was choking me to death with her big arms. Finally, I threw her off and came behind her back, but when I got there I realized my arms wouldn't fit around her. In desperation I began to shake her and pound her chest with my fists. She was turning purple. I gave her one final punch in the stomach. I knew I wasn't hurting her. Her stomach was like one of those fluffy but firm hotel pillows.

The punch had its desired effect. She heaved an enormous sigh that reminded me of King Kong. Then there was a rumbling reminiscent of the sound of waves building up on the eastern end of Long Island during hurricane season, and all of a sudden, a terrific recoil. I don't know what it sounds like when a volcano begins to spew lava, but I'll wager the rolling, undulating roar that emanated from Monica's stomach wasn't very far off, if only from the harmonic point of view. The bone cascaded out of her mouth along with what at first was a steady flow of vomit. The vomit looked like the cement that rolls down the chute of one of those big trucks with the rotating barrels. This initial even-handed outflow, which created a puddle in front of our television, then turned into a more violent spewing that covered the screen and all my exercise equipment. I was both aghast and relieved.

Finally, like all natural eruptions, the disturbance subsided—but not without one final blast of fury that landed right in my face, dripping down to soil my clothes. At first I'd held my arms out to her and exclaimed, "Thank God you're alive." When, however, her vomit hit me right in the face like a gale-force wind, my instinctive disgust overcame the feelings of gratitude and I began a violent heaving all my own. I vomited right back in her face, but considering my superior mobility, I was able to propel myself to the bathroom to prevent an even further mess. I must have thrown up for a half an hour. I won't say I felt cleansed. It's hard to feel cleansed when, after having had your head stuck in a filthy toilet bowl, you walk out to see an almost 300-pound woman sitting prostrate, marooned in the remains of your regurgitated life together.

We looked at each other. Monica still had vomit all over the flowery smock dress that she perpetually wore, and I thought to myself *what is she going to do? She loves that old smock dress, and I don't think they sell that style at Wal-Mart anymore.* I myself was no fashion plate. When I gazed at myself in the plastic heart-shaped mirror that hung on our living room wall, in which we used to see the image of our writhing naked bodies, I noticed that vomit had caked into my hair. I walked closer to Monica, navigating my way to avoid the especially slippery areas. If she hadn't been sitting in her own puddle of vomit, I might have plunked myself right down next to her. I actually contemplated the possibility until the fumes got to me and I started to gag. I couldn't afford to start up once more. I'd already had the dry heaves. There was nothing left inside of me. So, like Romeo calling to his beloved as he stood on the street below her balcony, I sang my praises at arms length. I told Monica I loved her. I told her that the stinking mess in our living room only reminded me how much I cared about her and valued our life together. I also mentioned that we were going to need to call a professional cleaning service.

Monica looked dazed. Like most couples, we had our routines, and as the days and weeks passed, we had taken each other for granted. I knew Monica would be there. She could barely move. In fact, I was aware she would always be sitting on the living room sofa with her usual tray table full of goodies, and besides leaving for a day or two to work with a touring company, the only place I went was to my regular AA meeting. Monica knew I could be counted on to end up at home at X, Y, or Z hour. The desire for alcohol had long left me, though my alcoholic thinking was still there—as they say, *I came for the drinking and stayed for the thinking*—and with the exception of that brief moment when Monica blew me, so had my desire for sex. Complacency had set in. But Monica's near-death experience had made it painfully clear how devastated I would have been if anything had happened to her. I still stumbled when it came to words. My caring feelings came out like little more than a slap on the wrist as I admonished her to chew more carefully, but I was worried. She ate too fast.

"I still have a sour taste in my throat. I need an Oreo or something before 'Judge Judy' comes on."

I wet a paper towel and cleaned off the screen of our TV. I turned up the volume, which we always do when one of our favorite programs is coming on. When I wiped away the vomit, we found ourselves in the middle of a commercial for Stay-Free Maxi Pads. Sometimes when Monica was watching, I wondered what she was thinking, since it was hard to detect the presence of emotion; the rolls of fat created a poker-face. She was so concentrated on the television that she'd already forgotten the mess in the apartment and the upchuck that covered her. And who was I to puncture her balloon? I got a small paper plate out of the kitchen cabinet and carefully laid three of the double-filled Oreos on it. And I brought her a glass of apple juice.

"Don't you have any of that ice-cold milk?" I would have brought her the cold milk she loved with cookies if her stomach hadn't been upset.

"I need a commitment. I need to know our relationship is going somewhere." *Next week Dawn confronts Robert on "One Life to Live."* I looked over in Monica's direction to see if she was connecting the soap opera star's words to our situation, but she simply stuck another Oreo in her mouth. Monica was like those prisoners who build walls of muscle (in her case it was fat) to protect themselves from emotional pain. She fortified herself with her constant eating. Monica picked up the remote and switched the channel. Bob Dole was sitting in a garden, hyping the virtues of Viagra.

"James, these cookies are so good. Could you bring me a few more? And I don't think a little milk would hurt me."

It was uncanny how she and I were always on the same wave length. She'd guessed exactly why I hadn't brought the milk without my explaining anything. It was this unspoken rapport that had existed in our relationship from the first days of our fucking, and continued on today. In addition, she hadn't called me by my Christian name in a long time. I was touched. For a moment, I played with the idea of moving us to a motel until the place could be cleaned up. Then I realized Monica was already adjusting to the new conditions. By the time we packed up and found a place to stay, we'd both miss our favorite programs. She seemed happy. The cleanup would simply have to be done around her. I could see Monica was working up an appetite already. Despite the fact I'd vomited my guts out, I needed to work out. We had an institutional-grade slop bucket and mop I kept on hand for just these kinds of emergencies. I filled it with warm water and soap and started to work on the most egregious puddles myself. As I looked at Monica I was filled with gratitude about the life we'd created together. Yes, I had a few bones to pick with her here and there and we had a big mess on our hands now, but these kinds of details are incidental when you're in love.

THE END